Darby looked over her shoulder in time to see the colt give a frisky buck before he trotted after Navigator. Then he nipped at the gelding's tail.

"You're in awfully good spirits for an orphan," Darby said. She patted Navigator's neck. "And you're a good boy for putting up with him."

The colt kept following them.

*This is great,* Darby thought. If he trailed after them all the way back to the ranch, someone might recognize him. Or Aunty Cathy, the ranch manager, could phone their neighbors.

Who *wouldn't* notice if they'd lost a cream-colored colt with turquoise eyes? But Darby couldn't help thinking, *Please don't belong to anyone else.*

Check out the

# Phantom Stallion

series, also by Terri Farley!

Read all the
*Phantom Stallion*
WILD HORSE ISLAND *adventures!*

# Phantom Stallion

## WILD HORSE ISLAND 4

## CASTAWAY COLT

### TERRI FARLEY

HarperTrophy®
*An Imprint of* HarperCollins*Publishers*

Harper Trophy® is a registered trademark of HarperCollins Publishers.

Castaway Colt

Copyright © 2008 by Terri Sprenger-Farley

Library of Congress catalog card number: 2007931753
ISBN 978-0-06-088617-2
Typography by Jennifer Heuer
❖
First Harper Trophy edition, 2008

# 4
# CASTAWAY COLT

©Gary Chalk

TWO SISTERS VOLCANOES

MESSAGE
BOTTLE LANDING

'IOLANI
RANCH

RAIN
FOREST

SUN
HOUSE

OLD PLANTATION

TUTU'S
COTTAGE

CRIMSON
VALE

NIGHT DIGGER
POINT BEACH

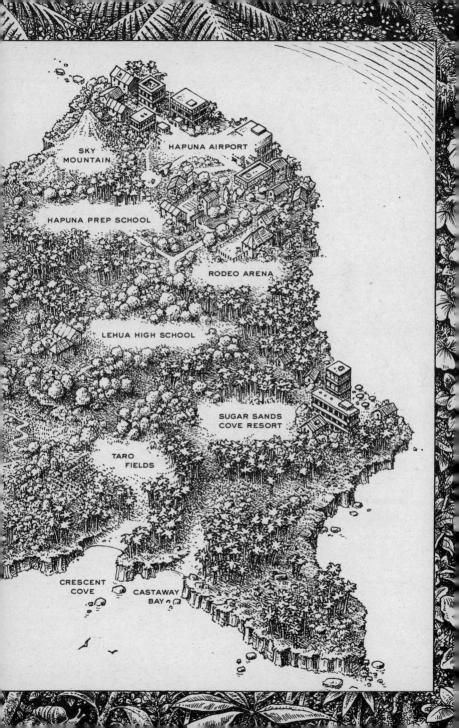

# 4
# CASTAWAY COLT

Chapter 1

Black sand muffled the sound of Navigator's hooves as he trotted toward the ocean.

Head flung high, the brown gelding breathed the salt of waves lapping up on Night Digger Point Beach.

Darby Carter could hardly believe her eyes. She'd grown up near the beach in California, but she'd never seen black sand. Did people who'd been raised on Hawaiian islands look at a dark coastline as an everyday thing?

"Just another day in paradise," Darby joked to her horse. "And you're already barefooted."

As she gazed out at the ocean, Darby couldn't wait to take off her riding boots and feel the millions of dark crystals work up between her toes.

Ever since Megan, Darby's first friend in Hawaii, had described Night Digger Point Beach, Darby had been eager to see it.

Today, the last day before starting her new school, was the perfect occasion to explore this black-sand beach.

The only thing that would have made the day even better was if she could have brought Hoku, her mustang, along with her. Darby had just spent a week in the rain forest with Hoku, and now she couldn't bear being away from the filly.

Begging to bring Hoku along because she loved her would not convince her grandfather, Jonah, to allow it. So she instead tried a more sensible approach.

"Wouldn't it be good training for me to pony Hoku to the beach? And if we had any little adventures"—Darby drew a quick breath, hoping Jonah wouldn't mention the strange stallions and wild pigs they'd encountered since they'd arrived on this wild island—"Hoku could learn from Navigator how to act."

To Darby, it had sounded like an excellent proposal, but Jonah hadn't seen it her way.

"What you call adventure, I call bad planning," Jonah had answered. "And the filly's too green to be mixed up in more of it."

"But—"

"You and Navigator have a good time, because there's work waiting for you when you get back," Jonah had said. "Unless you want to start working right now."

Darby had been about to protest that she'd finished all her chores when she caught the direction of Jonah's gaze.

He'd squinted pointedly toward Hoku's corral. There, the sorrel filly had touched noses over the fence with an old bay gelding named Judge.

Darby had known what Jonah's look meant, so she'd ridden away on Navigator.

Only now, on the beach, did she confide in her horse. "I don't know if what he wants is possible. Hoku lived as a wild horse. What do you think?" she asked, absently working her fingers through Navigator's black mane while she gazed at the ocean. "Can I make her loyal to me over you horses?"

Darby smiled as Navigator feinted a nip at her stirrup.

"Does that mean you're not into scenery?" she asked her horse, but Navigator turned back toward the waves with pricked ears.

The magical realm named for the night-digging sea turtles that used it as a nursery looked like another world.

Megan had had to go to school today, but she'd promised Darby that they'd pack a picnic supper on the Fourth of July, trek to this beach, and spend the night watching mother turtles dig black-sand cradles for their eggs.

Darby sighed. It sounded like fun, but this was April. She didn't know how much longer she'd be on Wild Horse Island. The Fourth of July seemed a long way off.

Navigator neighed, pawed up a shower of sand, then pulled at his bit, telling Darby he wanted to lope into the waves.

"No, the tide's coming in," Darby told her horse.

She could bodysurf and swim. She could spot rip-tides and escape their attempts to drag her out to sea, but she'd climbed onto a horse for the very first time just a few weeks ago. Riding waves on a boogie board was one thing; riding them on a horse was a test she wasn't ready for. Yet.

But then Darby noticed a foam-filled depression on top of a big rock. The rock was about five or six horse lengths away and only as high as Navigator's back.

As the foam turned into a mirror-clear surface, Darby longed to explore a Hawaiian tide pool and see if it had anemones, mussels, and little fish, like the tide pools in Southern California.

"If I ground-tie you, you'll stay put, right?" Darby asked Navigator.

She imagined dismounting, tugging off her boots, and picking her way up that slippery, truck-sized rock to the tide pool.

Waves rolled in and splashed over the boulder. Seawater filled the pool and overflowed in bubbly streamers.

As spray drifted on the breeze, misting Darby's face, she told herself the waves' impact wouldn't be enough to knock her off her feet.

Darby stood in her stirrups for a better view of the tide pool.

It was perfectly round.

"Either it was made with a giant ice-cream scoop," Darby told Navigator, "or a bubble popped there when the lava was cooling."

The big gelding stood still, his muscles tensed beneath the saddle, but Darby didn't think he was listening to her.

"Do you smell something interesting? Or see —" Darby stopped whispering.

She saw it, too.

Something moved. The creature must have been balanced on a ledge in the seaward side of the rock. It was as white as the sea foam. Maybe a giant bird?

But wait. That wasn't a wing.

No, a feathery *tail* switched over there. And it was followed by a colt-sized bottom.

Darby gave a surprised laugh. She'd only lived on 'Iolani Ranch for a few weeks, but she knew horses pulled themselves up with their front legs first.

*Not this little horse,* she corrected herself.

The foal obviously did things his own way. And

his way of standing up wasn't the most startling difference about him.

Wind blew tufts of mane into curls as the colt turned toward Darby. He studied her with wide, turquoise eyes.

Navigator made a determined yank at the bit, and this time Darby let him move closer.

*Hey, little guy.* Darby aimed her silent words toward the colt, but she didn't speak. If he was a wild horse, born into the herd in Crimson Vale, he might spook at her human sounds. She didn't want him to bolt into the ocean.

Navigator's strides stopped at the edge of the truck-sized rock.

Excitement switched Darby's senses on high. She saw the colt wasn't a new baby. At a guess, he was three or four months old, and his coat was a color not found in a box of crayons.

A blush of palomino shimmered among the colt's white hairs, reminding her of waxy white honeycomb.

His blue eyes were flecked with green.

*So that's why they look turquoise,* Darby thought. And though she'd read that many white mammals were blind at birth, the colt stared at her through a fringe of white eyelashes, telling her he could see her just fine.

The colt's narrow face reminded her of a Thoroughbred's. His rotating ears were the size of

Darby's cupped hands, telling her that he'd be a towering stallion someday.

But now he whisked his feather-duster tail from side to side and picked his sure-footed way around the volcanic rock.

Stopping just a few yards away, he pointed his pink nose up at Navigator and sniffed, considering horse and rider from this new angle.

"Hi, baby," Darby whispered, since he seemed unafraid.

Suddenly Navigator backed up. The colt might be fearless, but Navigator's move slammed Darby against the saddle's cantle. Her free arm swung behind her and she flattened her palm against the gelding's rump to steady herself.

"What's up?" she asked Navigator as he kept retreating from the colt.

The little creature followed, making jabs with its nose.

Navigator sidestepped the lips fluttering toward him.

"Are you hungry, baby?" Darby asked.

The white colt was searching for a meal. Navigator's nicker was gentle, but it was definitely a refusal.

"I'm afraid Navigator can't feed you," Darby said, but the white colt wasn't discouraged. He trotted after the gelding.

Darby surveyed the shore. Where was the colt's

mother? She saw no mare and heard no worried whinny over the rushing waves.

When the colt's spindly legs brought him near enough, he nudged Navigator's ticklish flank. The gelding snorted.

The colt was so close, Darby could have leaned down and moved him away with a push.

Instead, she touched her heels to Navigator's sides and the relieved gelding jogged off a few strides.

Darby looked over her shoulder in time to see the colt give a frisky buck before he trotted after Navigator. Then he nipped at the gelding's tail.

"You're in awfully good spirits for an orphan," Darby said. She patted Navigator's neck. "And you're a good boy for putting up with him."

The colt kept following them.

*This is great,* Darby thought. If he trailed after them all the way back to the ranch, someone might recognize him. Or Aunty Cathy, the ranch manager, could phone their neighbors.

Who *wouldn't* notice if they'd lost a cream-colored colt with turquoise eyes?

Darby gave a celebratory bounce in her saddle.

She'd almost ruled out the possibility that the colt was the offspring of the wild horses in Crimson Vale. It wasn't impossible, but in Nevada, Hoku's range-land home, Darby had learned that wild horses knew that safety was with the herd. Maybe this little colt had been separated from his band long enough that he'd decided Navigator and he could be a two-horse herd.

Darby shrugged, trying to figure out another reason for the colt to be alone. Maybe he *was* tame. He could have been wading in the shallows with his mother when a strong wave knocked him off his hooves.

After all, she'd just been thinking the waves might knock *her* down.

Too small to win against the currents, the colt could have been washed ashore here, on Night Digger Point Beach.

Or maybe he belonged to 'Iolani Ranch. He might have slipped out of the broodmare pasture. But that didn't make sense. She'd ridden those pastures for hours, memorizing the horses and their names. She'd remember a blue-eyed colt.

"Keep tagging along," Darby called back to the colt, and he did. For about ten minutes.

When Darby heard a thump in the sand, she looked back. The colt had stopped, folded his legs, and curled up in the sea grass. His head nodded until his whiskers touched his bent knees. Then he fell asleep.

Darby waited, and Navigator took the time to swing his head around to study this new annoyance.

Darby looked the colt over, too. He wasn't the cutest baby ever born, but once he grew into his head and hooves, he'd be a sleek, white beauty.

"You'll turn into a swan," Darby whispered, and the sound was enough to wake the colt from his nap.

"Let's go," Darby said.

Navigator moved into a swinging walk, but the colt was rested from his nap. He was even friskier now, and more of a bother to the big horse. Openmouthed, he darted after the gelding.

Darby clucked to her horse, but the colt had already grabbed Navigator's tail.

"Your mom hasn't taught you any manners yet, has she?" Darby asked.

Navigator stomped and whisked his black tail away from the colt's mouth.

"He's telling you that's a good way to get kicked," Darby warned as Navigator moved on.

To judge by his pretty prancing, the colt's feelings weren't hurt. Darby would have laughed if the colt's milk teeth hadn't clamped down hard on Navigator's tail again.

This time the gelding couldn't flick his tail loose.

Navigator's head swung around. Eyes narrowed, he clacked his teeth within an inch of the colt's face and the colt gave up his hold.

Darby did her best to settle into the calm state of mind that helped her to read horses.

Letting her eyelids sag and shoulders soften, Darby tried to be receptive.

*What's wrong, little one?* Like a flower opening to the sun, she was taking in all she could about the colt when he let loose a whinny so shrill, it soared over the rushing waves and fluttering of leaves.

The pale foal cried out in victory, not fear, and Darby decided that though he might be hungry and lonely, he might also be a bit of a brat.

"Don't pull so hard," Darby scolded the colt, but when he zoomed in an excited circle around Navigator, she couldn't be mad at him.

*Please don't belong to anyone else,* Darby thought.

Of course it was greedy to hope Navigator, Hoku, *and* this white sea-fairy of a foal could make up her own personal herd of horses, but Darby imagined that very thing.

Her daydreams were interrupted by a squeaky sound. She quickly recognized it as just a loose board in the old plantation house that was falling into ruins in the jungle. But when she looked back to speak a reassuring word to the colt, he was gone.

Chapter 2

Darby and Navigator searched the seashore, the nearby ohia trees, and the clumps of rocks and lichen-covered boulders, but they found nothing.

Disgusted with her inability to find a single hoof-print, Darby finally gave up and headed back to 'Iolani Ranch.

With each of Navigator's long strides, Darby became more worried.

How long could a colt go without food? At his age, did he need mare's milk? Could he nibble grass? What had frightened him away?

Darby sucked in her stomach as if she could vanish from the sight of anything lurking unseen in the foliage around her.

"It's possible," she teased Navigator, "that he gave up following us because you told him your tail wasn't a toy."

Darby looked at the sun shining through the trees. It was just early afternoon, but if she planned to ride back to the ranch and get help finding the colt, she'd better hurry.

When she clucked to Navigator, he understood she was asking him to head for home, and settled into a long-reaching lope.

Darby spotted the shape of a horseman on the horizon. It was Kimo, one of her grandfather's cowboys. She remembered when she'd first met Kimo in the Hapuna Airport. She'd thought he was built as sturdy and square as a stone house. He was a burly young guy, but it turned out there was nothing rock-hard about Kimo except his muscles. His white smile and friendliness always made her feel at home.

Kimo didn't consider himself a real paniolo—as the best Hawaiian cowboys were called—but Darby didn't see why.

Now, for instance, she hadn't seen his hands move Conch's reins, but he'd invisibly signaled the grulla gelding into a dusty cow-horse stop that ended with Conch standing nose to tail beside Navigator.

"You tired out already?" Kimo asked.

His question might have hurt if it hadn't been for his grin, and the secret Darby knew.

Last week, Megan had overheard Kimo and Kit,

the ranch foreman, refer to Darby as "one smart, can-do *keiki*," or the "can-do kid."

"I'm not tired. I found this amazing white colt. He's following me—" Darby paused when Kimo peered past her. "I mean, he was. Really, just like 'Mary Had a Little Lamb,' but he took off."

"Yeah?"

Did the deepening sun wrinkles around Kimo's eyes indicate disbelief or amusement?

"Yeah," she said adamantly. "A young colt, like maybe three months old, I'm guessing, and he didn't look old enough to be out there alone."

"Out where?"

"Night Digger Point Beach."

"I'll go see what I can find," Kimo said.

Assuming he'd mistakenly said *I* instead of *we*, Darby turned Navigator to follow.

"Nope," Kimo said, shaking his head. "Cathy told me to send you home to try on gym clothes."

Darby was grateful that Aunty Cathy, the ranch manager and sort of her stand-in mother at 'Iolani Ranch, was handy with a needle and willing to alter her daughter Megan's outgrown gym clothes. Darby had already spent the money her mother had sent on new boots, so she was glad her gym uniform would be free.

But why should she quit riding and go back now? It couldn't take longer than five minutes to try on shorts and a T-shirt.

"That is, if I saw you," Kimo said.

Darby caught Kimo's shrug as he squinted into a breeze scented with ferns and flowers.

"Too bad you didn't see me," Darby said with an answering shrug.

Then she sent Navigator off at a jog, leading Kimo to the spot where she'd last seen the white colt.

Together, Darby and Kimo searched a stand of ohia trees that looked different from others she'd seen. Sparse as wizards' staffs thrust into the ground, they provided a promising hiding place, but the colt wasn't there.

They followed hoofprints to a stretch of black-sand beach covered with multicolored rocks. From pewter gray to salt white and coppery brown, they'd been pounded by the ocean until they were smooth and round as cobblestones. Neither Darby nor Kimo thought the colt would try to cross that loose surface if he had a chance to walk elsewhere.

At the edge of a damp forest, Darby saw shell-shaped fungus clinging to tree trunks. She mistook white globs on some rocks as far-flung sea foam until she rode close enough to see that it was some sort of lichen.

After hours of searching, Kimo finally told her to ride on back to the ranch.

"I'll keep looking until dark," he promised.

Darby knew he would, but if tomorrow hadn't

been her first day at a new school, she wouldn't have ridden back alone.

Sweaty and frustrated, Darby rode up from the broodmare pastures to the ranch yard.

Megan was already home from soccer practice. She could tell because the brown Land Rover with the 'Iolani Ranch owl painted on the door was parked in front of Sun House, and Peach, the Australian shepherd who rode shotgun each time anyone drove into town, wasn't waiting in his usual seat. *The next time the Land Rover goes to town, I'll be riding shotgun,* Darby thought.

Her stomach gave a nervous twist. Darby knew she was silly not to be looking forward to school.

She was a good student, so it shouldn't matter if eighth grade was part of the high school here.

"I'll do fine," Darby muttered to Navigator.

Navigator's coffee-colored head bobbed along with his steps. He'd enjoyed the workout, Darby thought. She patted his neck in thanks for his good-natured energy in searching for the white colt. She wished they'd found him, but she had faith that Kimo would.

Darby unsaddled Navigator and started brushing the dried sweat from his coat. She looked down the road, past the fox cages. Judge was still standing at Hoku's corral fence.

The old bay horse belonged to Mrs. Allen, the owner of Blind Faith Mustang Sanctuary and the

Dream Catcher Wild Horse Camp in Nevada.

When the ranch horse had been born, who would have guessed he'd end up in Hawaii? But Darby had adopted Hoku and brought her to Wild Horse Island, and Mrs. Allen had sent Judge along so that Hoku had a stablemate for her voyage.

On their arrival at the ranch, Jonah had told Darby not to let Hoku choose Judge—or any other horse—over her.

Since then, Judge had been grazing with other horses in one of the lower pastures.

According to Kit and Kimo, though, while Darby and Hoku had been in the rain forest last week, Judge's longing neighs had been endless. Somehow he'd known Hoku was gone.

Since their return, Judge had plodded up the hill to visit the mustang filly several times each day.

Now, Darby checked Navigator's hooves, thanked him for not picking up rocks, and gave him a shoulder pat that told him to move off and look for dinner.

Then Darby hung up her saddle, left her saddle blanket to air, hooked her bridle on its hanger, and strode down the road toward Judge.

"Get away!" Darby called to the old horse, but she must not have sounded any scarier than she felt.

Judge gazed at her as if he must have misunderstood. Darby pretended to scoop up a rock to throw at him.

The sweet old horse just tilted his ears forward,

trying to understand, until she felt a guilty ache.

"Shoo," Darby said, then fluttered her hands toward Judge.

Judge greeted her with a low rumble, and when she got close enough that Hoku switched her attention to Darby's odd gestures, Judge rolled his eyes and jogged away.

Hoku neighed after him, but the old bay kept moving.

"Hey, pretty girl," Darby said.

She smooched at the sorrel filly, counting the seconds until Hoku turned back.

Hoku's ears swiveled toward Darby like delicate golden leaves turning to the sun.

Darby sighed, took a quick look around to be sure no one was watching, then tightened her ponytail.

Hoku rushed to the fence. Her coppery chest pressed against the rails until Darby held out her hand. Then Hoku eased her head over the top rail.

"Our secret." Darby mouthed the words, but didn't say them loud enough for even Hoku to hear.

She'd only known for a week that the filly would come to her when she tightened her ponytail.

She loved the secrecy of it, and the idea that Hoku had chosen this silent signal.

Hoku dusted her lips over Darby's palm, then snorted, as if clearing an unwelcome scent from her nostrils.

"Don't tell me you can smell that colt," Darby said. "Besides, you'd like him. You two could play together."

As soon as she'd said the words, Darby reconsidered. Hoku already had a horse pal: Judge. If Darby supplied her with an equine playmate like the white colt, what would Hoku need with a human friend?

"Joking," Darby whispered.

After feeding the filly, she headed toward Sun House, eager to tell Megan, Jonah, and Aunty Cathy about the white colt.

In the entrance hall, Darby tugged off Megan's scuffed burgundy boots and added them to the pile of shoes that Megan, Cathy, and Jonah had lined up, toes to the wall.

Something fragrant wafted from the kitchen, but Darby passed it to check out the noise in the living room.

A television news broadcast provided background for conversation, but Darby knew no one would mind if she announced *her* news.

Megan and Aunty Cathy hadn't noticed her yet when Darby began, "Hey, you'll never believe—"

Aunty Cathy bit through a thread from the final stitch of her sewing, held up a pair of red shorts, and asked, "What do you think?"

Struggling to focus on the favor Aunty Cathy had done for her, instead of the colt, Darby said, "Wow, thanks."

Lehua High's school colors of red and gold were still eye-catching on the much-washed shorts and gold T-shirt sitting atop a stack of freshly folded clothes.

"I don't know that I'd go so far as a 'wow,'" Aunty Cathy said, laughing, "but you're welcome. And they'll do for the rest of the semester."

"Hey," Megan greeted Darby. The older girl sat cross-legged in front of the television, but her gaze was focused on the textbook in her lap.

"Hey," Darby answered. "You'll never guess what I—"

Megan glanced up, smiled, and asked, "Are you excited about tomorrow?"

"Sure." Darby tried her best not to sound impatient.

"Not nervous?"

"No," Darby fibbed.

"The best thing about school is that you get a fresh start every year," Aunty Cathy pointed out.

Tomorrow *would* have been a fresh start, Darby thought, if Megan—star forward on her soccer team—hadn't missed an important game.

The team had lost.

*You should have heard all my teammates. They wouldn't stop harassing me until I told them the whole stupid story,* Megan had said, rolling her eyes as she'd explained to Darby that instead of taking the blame in silence, she'd admitted she'd missed the game because she'd had to make sure her city-slicker houseguest—Darby—hadn't broken her neck after jumping off a cliff to rescue a horse.

Darby hoped the students at Lehua High School had more to do with their brain cells than remember her name.

"Here comes the story we've been waiting for," Megan said suddenly. "It's something about a missing horse."

A missing horse? On the news? Darby's mind started making connections.

"Hey, I bet—"

But Aunty Cathy was already shouting, "Jonah! You'll want to see this!"

"I won't," his booming voice insisted, but Darby heard her grandfather padding down the hall.

Darby was surprised to see him. Jonah usually worked until Kimo had left for the day and Cade and Kit had gone to the foreman's house for dinner.

Rubbing his wet hair with a towel, her grandfather pointed at Darby. "Why didn't you see off that old gelding that was bothering your filly?"

"I did," Darby said, confused.

"Good," Jonah answered, then left the towel hanging around his neck as he faced the television's scratchy picture. "Now hush."

As they all stared at the screen in silence, Darby made out a surfer gliding along a white-tipped wave and the sound of strumming ukuleles.

"What's that got to do with a lost horse?" Jonah grumbled.

"It'll be on after the commercial," Aunty Cathy said. She was standing, but she didn't leave the room.

"They showed Babe in the little preview thing," Megan assured Jonah.

"Dressed like an angel." Jonah's sarcasm suggested that he didn't consider his sister angelic.

"Everything up at Sugar Sands Cove is white. It's their signature color," Megan explained. "I think it's cool."

"Cool," Jonah repeated. "My big sister is very cool when it comes to money."

Darby's brow tightened in a frown, but she kept quiet. She hadn't yet met her wealthy great-aunt.

"Makes me crazy up there," Jonah muttered. "And now she's got the *pupule* idea that throwing away money will make her more."

Aunty Cathy handed Darby the gym clothes, but kept her eyes focused on the television as she said, "Sometimes it's true that you've got to spend money to make money."

"But those tourist rides," Jonah grumbled.

Tourist rides at Sugar Sands Cove or 'Iolani Ranch? Darby wondered. 'Iolani was a working ranch, and Darby had figured out that every hour of every day was needed to keep it running. Just as she was about to ask for details, the news came back on.

"A Moku Lio Hihiu innkeeper makes an appeal for the return—"

"Innkeeper." Jonah sneered, but this time both Megan and Aunty Cathy shushed him.

"—and tells how a valuable cremello foal was swept overboard during a struggle with the sea . . ."

The screen was filled with the vivacious, concerned face of a Hawaiian woman with short, shingled hair and slick mango-colored lipstick.

"I just hope he's okay. He's such a baby," she said.

"Babe Kealoha Borden is best known for the world-class Sugar Sands Cove Resort, which she opened with her internationally famous polo-player husband . . ."

So that was her great-aunt Babe, Darby thought.

The reporter's voice continued as photographs showed Babe in gauzy white, floating through the plush rooms and lavish gardens of her resort, which then dissolved into a shot of her as a flower-bedecked parade rider.

". . . is also known for her love of horses. 'My mare Flight foaled while she was on Maui for training,'" Babe said on-screen. "'When Stormbird, her colt, was ready to travel, they started for home. . . .'" Babe's voice trailed off and Darby heard the breaking of waves in the background. "'Rough water came out of nowhere. My grandson brought the horses up on deck so that they'd be safer in case the storm turned worse.'"

The reporter's dramatic voice picked up the story, saying, "The storm did turn worse. The boat capsized. And though Flight was saved due to what Borden describes as Yawn's heroic actions—"

"Oh, gag me," Megan muttered.

Darby caught just a glimpse of a Nordic-looking guy with blond hair, blue eyes, in openmouthed laughter as he hauled on ropes in what might be a sailboat race. He must be about college age, Darby thought, and he sure didn't look worthy of Megan's scorn. Or the name Yawn.

"—little Stormbird jumped into the rough seas between Maui and Moku Lio Hihiu, and is presumed lost."

When the camera returned to Babe, she held up a photograph.

Darby's heart beat faster. She squinted, trying to see better, but the camera lens was dazzled by star flashes that came from Babe's diamond rings as she went on. "He didn't drown," Babe insisted. She faced the camera with a determination that made Darby glance at Jonah. Chic clothes and elegant manners couldn't hide the family stubbornness. "He's come ashore somewhere, and I'm counting on your viewers' spirit of aloha to help find him."

As the reporter came back on, he joked, "The aloha spirit is not all the Bordens are counting on. The family has offered a substantial reward for the safe return of little Stormbird."

In khaki pants and Hawaiian shirt, the reporter stood next to a palm tree on Sugar Sands Cove's grounds.

He held up a poster of a check showing a figure with more zeroes than Darby could make sense of right away, but she heard the reporter ask, "Isn't that a lot to pay for such a young horse of unproven worth?"

"His worth is proven to me," Babe said, crossing her arms.

"You can see more photographs of Sugar Sands Cove Resort and learn the details of this amazing offer on our website . . . "

Darby didn't hear another word, because the camera zoomed in on a color photograph of Flight and Stormbird.

Small and pale, the colt would have been hard to make out, standing next to his snow-white mother, except for one spot of color.

The colt looked out of the television with turquoise eyes.

 Chapter 3

"That's him!" she gasped.

"Shh!" Megan, Aunty Cathy, and Jonah all said, still staring at the television, but Darby couldn't hold in her excitement any longer.

"No, you've got to listen. That colt I told you about—he's Stormbird. I found him!"

"Darby, honey, when exactly did you tell us about this colt?" Aunty Cathy asked.

"Now." Darby took a deep breath. "Since I came in, I've been trying to!"

"Speak up, then," Jonah said.

"We found him on Night Digger Point Beach, and then he followed us—"

"'We'?" Megan asked.

"Me and Navigator. And Kimo's still out looking for him."

"And he looked like that colt?" Megan gestured toward the television. She was as excited as Darby.

"He *is* that colt," Darby insisted, but her words became giggles as Megan jumped to her feet, keeping her arms wrapped around her ribs as if she was trying to contain her delight.

Darby could see that if it was up to Megan, the two of them would be leaping onto horses and galloping toward Night Digger Point Beach right now.

But Jonah reined them both in. "Tell me why you're so sure it's not some other colt," he asked.

"His eyes are blue," Darby said, "and his coat is creamy white. Oh, and his nose is pink," Darby added, recalling how the colt had looked up to study her.

"Cremellos have pink skin," Cathy said, "not black, like white Andalusians and Arabs."

"Too fancy for me," Jonah scoffed, but Darby saw a slow smile lift one side of his black mustache. Then her grandfather laughed out loud. "Good. Sounds like we'll be keeping that money in the family."

"And you say you know where he is?" Aunty Cathy sounded cautious.

"Why didn't you bring the colt in?" Jonah asked.

"I know where he *was*," Darby explained.

"Tango will find him!" Megan interrupted.

That was a great idea, Darby thought. Megan's rose roan mare would have perfect instincts for the task. Tango had been a wild horse, then a captive one. She'd been trained, then freed by an accident, and now she was home again.

But Jonah hadn't gotten that far in the plan. "You say Kimo's out looking for him right now," Jonah mused.

"I would have kept searching with him, but he told me Aunty Cathy wanted me to try on my gym clothes," Darby said as Aunty Cathy walked, smiling, toward the kitchen.

"Gym clothes!" Megan shook her head in disbelief, and then she was on her feet, practically dancing as she slung an arm around Darby's shoulders.

"If Kimo doesn't find him, Darby—my old buddy, old pal—I'll help you. And we'll split the money!"

"Dinner's ready," Aunty Cathy called.

"Mom!" Megan yelled at the wall between the living room and kitchen. "We've got to go find Stormbird!"

"Kimo will bring him, if he's out there," Aunty Cathy shouted back.

Darby couldn't help looking at Jonah.

"I know it's him," Darby persisted. "He's the right age and everything."

"And how many white colts with blue eyes are out wandering around alone?" Megan asked Jonah, then wheeled on Darby. "He was by himself, right?"

"Yes," Darby said. "And lonesome, too. He wanted to play with Navigator."

Aunty Cathy returned. Carrying a platter loaded with food, she sidled in between the two girls and indicated that they should follow her to the table on the lanai.

"Pineapple chicken with sticky rice, stir-fried red and yellow peppers, broccoli, and—"

"Mom, we've got to go right now!"

"It's dinnertime."

"So?" Megan's gestures were huge with frustration, and Darby could see Jonah's amusement. "I'll be able to buy you dinner every night for a month, two months—"

"Simmer down, Megan," Aunty Cathy said. "It will be dark soon."

Megan's eyes beseeched Darby to help, and Darby would have, except that Aunty Cathy caught Megan's silent plea for reinforcements. She pointed at Jonah and Darby, and snapped, "You two, sit down."

Darby did as she was told. Jonah pretended to flinch, then settled at his place.

"You knew about this," Aunty Cathy said to Jonah as he began to eat.

"About the colt and reward," he admitted. "But I never guessed he was alive. Or nearby."

Darby ate, but her right foot jiggled back and forth with barely controlled energy. She was glad no one could see, because she couldn't seem to stop it.

"Babe *was* going to offer a week at the resort, instead of money," Jonah told them. "But she's afraid . . . How did she put it? That 'someone unsavory might win.'"

Aunty Cathy put down her fork and sat back in her chair. "You know what that means."

Darby didn't think it was very hard to figure out. What if a kid like her found the colt? She'd never been to a luxury hotel and she wouldn't know how to act there. Besides, she'd rather have the money.

Taking Hoku back to the mainland—she winced at the thought—would be awfully expensive. And boarding her . . .

*One thing at a time,* Darby told herself, and tried not to think about going back.

"What are you guys thinking about that you're not saying?" Megan asked, looking between Jonah and her mother.

"You're not going out after dark," Aunty Cathy said, in a tone that put off any discussion.

Megan poked at a chunk of chicken and looked sideways at Darby. What should they do? Wait until tomorrow, after school?

There was too much to think about. Her classes, the "surprise" student Megan couldn't wait to introduce her to, remembering her locker combination, finding her way around the campus . . .

She really hoped Kimo found the colt tonight.

❈ ❈ ❈

Only five minutes later, Kimo knocked on the door, opened it, and leaned his head inside.

"Couldn't find your little sea horse. Sorry," he called in apology, and Darby's heart fell.

"Come in, Kimo. Eat something," Cathy encouraged him.

The cowboy clomped in, but stopped at the edge of the lanai and shook his head. "Gotta have dinner with my dad. Not that it will be anything that looks as good as that."

"You can take some with you," Cathy persisted, but she stopped when the phone began ringing.

Jonah stood up, but he turned to Kimo. "No sign of it?"

"Plenty of signs," Kimo said. "But no colt. I'm guessing it has a little hidey-hole somewhere, a little spit of land, yeah? The freshest tracks I saw led into the water."

The phone was still ringing, and though Megan usually jumped up to answer it, this time she leaned forward with her elbows on the table, eager to hear everything Kimo said.

When Kimo paused, Megan slapped her palms on the table and said, "I'm going down to Night Digger Point Beach. Right now."

"You're staying here to help Darby decide what to wear to school tomorrow," her mother corrected her.

"No way!" Megan said, but when her sharp tone

made the others turn from the mother-daughter argument as if they were embarrassed, Megan apologized. "I'm sorry, Mom, but Darby can try on clothes after dark. Right now Stormbird is probably starving!"

"Is anyone going to answer that phone?" Jonah asked.

"He *was* nudging Navigator like he wanted to nurse," Darby said, darting a quick glance at Aunty Cathy. "I guess that means he's hungry."

*See?* Megan's expression said, but she had the good judgment not to push her point.

"If Kimo couldn't find him, what makes you think you can?" Aunty Cathy asked.

"Aloha, folks," Kimo said, edging back toward the front door. "Headin' for home now."

As Jonah walked out with Kimo, Darby's stomach knotted with frustration. If she were having this argument with her own mother, she'd jump in and fight, but she didn't know Aunty Cathy quite that well yet.

Instead, she took a long drink of water and wondered why the caller was letting the phone ring for so long.

"I'll find the colt, because *I'm* taking a real horse charmer with me," Megan answered her mother.

Darby tried to swallow her water, but she ended up choking. Not that anyone noticed.

Aunty Cathy crossed her arms, looking as stubborn as Megan did hopeful.

"I'll get the phone," Darby said when she could draw a breath, but just then Jonah strode back indoors and beat her to it.

Aunty Cathy and Megan settled into a cranky silence. Though Darby felt uneasy, she didn't go hide in her room, because it felt like there might still be a chance to go after Stormbird.

"If he thinks that gives him a passport to cross my borders and come onto my land . . ." Jonah's voice boomed from the kitchen.

Then he snorted.

"Sure. Sure he does," Jonah said. He was quiet for a full minute before he said, "Yeah, okay. Aloha."

They heard him moving around in the kitchen, slamming a pan in the sink, running water, and muttering in Hawaiian.

Darby heard only one word she understood: *pupule*, which she was pretty sure meant "crazy."

No one moved until Jonah came back out on the lanai.

"It's sad to say when you haven't even met her yet," Jonah told Darby, "but your aunty Babe is deranged."

"She is?" Darby asked.

"Not really," Cathy said. "Babe is my friend as well as Jonah's sister, and though they're as different as siblings can be, she is not deranged."

"I wouldn't be too sure," Jonah said, and Darby would have laughed, but there was no humor in her grandfather's voice as he added, "She talked to Manny. He's promised to locate the colt."

Aunty Cathy drew in a loud breath, then said, "Maternal instinct." She shook her finger at the girls and said, "I knew there was a reason you weren't going out tonight."

Megan looked down and so did Darby. Manny was Cade's stepfather. A cruel man who trafficked in stolen Hawaiian treasures, he had no qualms about breaking the law.

No matter how determined they were to find Stormbird, neither Megan nor Darby was eager to stumble upon Manny in the dark.

"You know what she said, your friend Babe?" Jonah asked Cathy. "She told me the colt's story, and how the reward meant free publicity for the resort, even though money could bring out the worst in people. Then she said, about Manny, 'He is violent; I don't like that about him, but he'll get the job done.'"

Maybe it was just the cold way Jonah delivered the words, but Babe didn't sound very nice, Darby thought.

Darby's worries were underlined by Jonah's silence as he stared off the lanai and into the dusk falling over 'Iolani Ranch.

Talking about clothes didn't hold either girl's attention even though they'd gone to Darby's bedroom so that she could model her next day's wardrobe. Neither of them could help talking about Stormbird instead.

"If Aunt Babe likes Stormbird enough to offer a huge reward for him, why isn't she out looking for him herself?" Darby asked.

"She can't leave the resort, I guess," Megan told her.

"If she's rich, it seems like she'd have a manager or something to run things," Darby said. "Or her husband. She's married, right?"

"Yeah." Megan drew the word out as if she wasn't quite convinced it was true.

"So?"

"I'm not sure how much I should fill you in on your Hawaiian family," Megan said.

Darby waited patiently. Turning away from Megan so the older girl wouldn't feel like she was being cross-examined, Darby picked a brown leaf off her lucky bamboo plant.

"See, Babe's husband Phillipe is a polo player, and he keeps most of his horses on Oahu and, uh, someplace in Argentina, I think, because those are the places where he plays polo. . . . "

Wow, who married a polo player? Darby wondered. It sounded so glamorous.

"Babe used to go with him, sometimes," Megan said, "but not anymore, since your cousins came to live with her."

Darby pivoted away from the lucky bamboo to face Megan.

"I have a cousin?"

"Two," Megan said, holding up two fingers.

"Why didn't anyone ever tell me this?"

"I just did."

"I know, but . . ." Darby paused, waiting for her mind to stop spinning. "This is so weird. I lived in Pacific Pinnacles, in Los Angeles County, where there are thousands, maybe millions of people I could be related to; I mean, the odds are better—but it was just my mom, my dad, and . . ." Darby shook her head. "Then I come to this dinky little island—which I love," she rushed to assure Megan, "and I'm related to everyone."

"Not me," Megan chirped.

"No, but just about. I call your mom aunty."

Megan laughed until Darby stopped her with another question. "So why do my cousins live with Babe? Does their whole family?"

"Just them, right now," Megan said. "It's just, Babe's daughter did the same thing she did—"

"Their mom. My other aunt. Or second cousin, or whatever," Darby said, changing back into jeans and a T-shirt.

"She married a guy known as White Water Willie, a kayaker who started surfing, and he competes all over the world. But the kids needed a home base, a place to go to school, so Babe took them in.

Although one's away at college on the mainland."

"Amazing. And the other one is one of my surprises for tomorrow?" Darby guessed.

"Yep," Megan said.

"That will be really fun," Darby said.

Megan shifted uncomfortably on the edge of Darby's bed as if she was about to say something else, but then the phone rang again. And this time, Megan made a dash for it.

The call was for Darby.

Ellen Kealoha Carter, Darby's mother, had phoned to tell her daughter that the film she was shooting in Tahiti was running behind schedule.

"We've been having these fierce tropical storms," Ellen shouted, and even though she was inside her trailer on the film set when she added, "They're brutal," Darby could barely hear her over the hammering rain.

"I just wanted you to know." Her mother sounded melancholy. "It could mean a few extra weeks."

"It's okay, Mom," Darby said. "But I do miss you. A lot."

A sudden thought bobbed to the surface of Darby's mind. Because she had to give it a minute to take shape, she said, "Mom, cover your other ear and just listen for a minute. I have something cool to tell you."

For ten full minutes, Darby described Night

Digger Point Beach—which her mother remembered with a longing sigh—and the white colt she'd found there. She told her mother that the colt belonged to Babe Borden's mare, and then she announced the reward.

Darby only detoured from her story to answer, as well as she could, her mother's questions about her aunt Babe.

Her mother said, "Sounds like you're getting a lot more excitement than you did in Pacific Pinnacles. I hope home won't be too tame for you." It was then that Darby knew what she'd do with the reward money.

"When I get the reward, I'll fly you over for a visit," Darby said.

"That's great, honey." Her mother sounded like she was just humoring her.

"Mom, I *am* going to catch him," Darby insisted.

"Your grandfather must be doing something right. You're getting quite the imagination over there. I hope you're writing all this down."

"I am," Darby said slowly. But why wasn't her mother taking her seriously?

"Darby, I believe you," her mother said. As usual, she was pretty good at reading Darby's silence. "It's just that—how are you going to catch a colt? Sure, it's a small island, but it could run you ragged along the coastline and you'd be wheezing. . . ."

"My asthma is so much better," Darby protested,

but her mother didn't seem to hear.

"Let's say the colt isn't wild. You haven't learned to rope, have you? Honey, you've only been riding a short time, and even newborn colts can be hard to handle."

Ellen had spent years hiding her ranch upbringing from her daughter, and Darby hadn't stopped being surprised when her mother said something like that, indicating that she knew a lot more about horses than she let on for twelve and a half years.

"I know. You're right," Darby told her mother.

But Darby knew she could do it. That night she wrote out plans on a piece of notebook paper. She'd just made a note to learn how much it would cost to fly her mother from Tahiti to Wild Horse Island, when Darby realized she wasn't just hoping for a visit.

At heart, she wanted her mother and Jonah to set aside their problems and have a warm reunion.

Darby stared up at the black rectangle of window over her bed.

If her mother and Jonah got along, maybe they could all live here! 'Iolani Ranch belonged to the Kealoha family. Jonah had built the little tree house atop Sun House just so that her mother would have separate quarters if she ever came back home.

Darby waggled her pencil between her pointer and middle fingers, and bit her lip.

*Would Mom agree to live this far away from Hollywood? Probably not.*

Feeling a quick stab of guilt as she thought of Heather, her best friend in Pacific Pinnacles, Darby realized she wasn't even sure that was what *she* wanted.

But here there were rainbows and waterfalls, rain forests and green rolling hills for Hoku to gallop over. . . .

Darby shook her head free of those images. She folded the list and slipped it into the diary stashed under her bed. Then she turned off her light and told herself that what she *really* wanted now was to grab as much sleep as she could so that tomorrow, at her new school, she would be brilliant.

 Chapter 4

Darby stared at the inside of her eyelids. She felt like she'd been mulling over her first day at Lehua High School forever.

Should she wear her hair up in a ponytail, or down loose? Should she get up now so that she'd have plenty of time to decide?

Her room was dark, but the glowing numbers on her bedside clock said 4:22. The clock, which had an awful, squawking alarm, was a gift from Megan. "Misery loves company," she'd teased, adding that she was glad she'd have Darby's company on the drive to school now.

She and Megan were getting to be good friends, but what if Megan's school friends hated Darby

Carter and Megan pretended she barely knew this geeky new girl?

Sun House was silent.

Lehua High School couldn't be as big as her old school, but what if she got lost? Or couldn't open her locker?

Darby rolled over on her back. She made her muscles go floppy, let her hands curl at her sides as she drew a gentle breath, then exhaled twice. She did it four times, because her mother, who was totally devoted to yoga, swore that such breathing smoothed out the most tangled thoughts.

Darby opened one eye. The clock said four thirty.

This was stupid. She might as well get up and go feed Hoku and Francie the fainting goat. But if she went outside now, she'd disturb the dogs. They'd bark and wake Kit and Cade.

Or she could go shower, but she'd probably wake Jonah. And later, she'd get hay all over her clothes and in her hair.

At last, she pulled on some work clothes and tip-toed down the hall. She opened the front door and held her breath, but she only heard the humming of the refrigerator. She slipped outside.

As she passed the dogs' kennel, Jack came out to stare at her. He clawed halfheartedly at the chain-link fence, then turned around and settled back to sleep with a grunt.

*Good dog*, Darby thought, and kept walking.

It soothed her to go inside Hoku's corral with an armload of hay and feed her filly that way.

The sweet nudges and gentle whuffling of horse lips over her arms and neck weren't all for the food. Some of them were affectionate gestures just for her.

By the time Hoku had eaten all of her hay, Darby was feeling happy and optimistic about the day ahead.

*Animals just make me happy,* Darby thought. *Hoku doesn't notice how I walk or talk or wear my hair. Why can't everyone be as kind and accepting as horses and dogs?*

And goats, she remembered with a start.

She forced herself to leave Hoku, bolted the corral gate behind her, and filled a bucket with Francie's breakfast. Once she'd done her morning dance with the playful black-and-white goat, Darby ran toward the house.

Time was slipping away.

As soon as she was back inside Sun House, Jonah called to her from the lanai.

"Granddaughter," he said.

Jonah gestured her out onto the wooden deck that overlooked the ranch, but he didn't ask if she'd fed Hoku, or if she was up early because she was nervous. He just stood beside her. Together they watched a searing gold edge of sun peek over the hills.

Darby let out a long breath and leaned against the lanai's rail. Whatever happened at school, at least she'd come home to this.

"If you want to go looking for this colt, take Jill and Peach with you."

Darby nodded. Jill and Peach were two of the ranch's five Australian shepherds. She'd memorized their names along with those of Jack, Sass, and Bart, with help from Kit. The Nevada cowboy had told her he found it easier to remember the dogs by their talents.

Jack and Jill were both black and helped gather and drive cattle, but Jill was suspicious of strangers. Sass's coat was a combination of black and white called blue merle, and because he was especially good with adult horses, he trotted out with Kit and Kimo more than the other dogs.

Bart was only a year old, black except for brown eyebrows and white boots. He'd been given to Jonah by the Zinks. He was an example of what went wrong with a dog that was bred to work, but kept as a house pet, Jonah said.

Bart had only two expressions: impish or ashamed. Darby had the feeling the young dog was on probation, and that Jonah wouldn't have kept him if Cade hadn't dedicated himself to making the pup a good ranch dog.

Peach was man's best friend. Jonah called him a red merle, but he looked pale orange and white to Darby. Peach considered himself a member of the family. His heart shone through adoring brown eyes, and if he wasn't asleep in the truck, he trailed whoever was doing the least active work.

"Too bad you can't take your attack horse," Jonah joked, "but the dogs will have to do."

Hoku wasn't an attack horse, but Darby knew what Jonah meant. She'd seen Hoku's mustang instincts come down on Black Lava, the wild stallion, and a rabid boar.

"I don't know the dogs' commands really well," Darby said.

"Hmph." Jonah flashed her a skeptical look. "You learn without trying. You've got a brain like—what's that stuff?—Velcro."

Darby swallowed, speechless for a few seconds. Before she found the words to thank her grandfather, he looked away from her.

Staring over the pastures again, he added, "You know plenty. You just forget to use it."

Darby crossed her arms and felt an unexpected spate of back talk about to escape her lips.

She was saved from such a lapse in judgment when a harsh sound surprised them both.

"Sounds like someone stepped on a duck," Jonah observed.

"It's my alarm!" Darby said.

She ran to her bedroom to silence it. It really was time to get ready for school.

By the end of her first day of school, the faces of two of Darby's teachers—Miss Day and Coach

Roffmore—and two of her classmates—Ann Potter and Duxelles, a scary girl who happened to be her cousin—would be tattooed on her mind forever.

But Darby didn't know that when Aunty Cathy dropped her and Megan off in front of the school and threw them a kiss good-bye.

"You look great. Stop fidgeting," Megan muttered to Darby as they came onto the campus of Lehua High School.

Darby had brushed her black hair until it was ruler-straight, then pushed it back over her shoulders. She wore tiny shell-shaped earrings that matched her pink polo shirt. Along with her jeans, she wore something she never would have worn at home: smooth leather boots, the color of brown sugar.

"Are you looking at everyone's feet?" Megan asked as they walked.

"No, just watching where I'm going," Darby answered, but that wasn't quite true, so she whispered, "So far I haven't I haven't seen one other girl wearing boots."

"That's because you haven't met Ann yet," Megan told her. "But you will soon."

"Ann," Darby repeated as Megan searched the students around them. "Is she mystery girl number one that you're introducing me to?"

"Yeah," Megan said, slipping past a group of guys who were carrying skateboards. "You two have so much in common. You're in the same grade, you both love horses, and I can't wait for you to find out her hometown."

Her hometown? Megan smiled at Darby's confusion, then rushed her along. "We need to hurry. The office is always crowded, and it'll be worse than usual because it's the first day of the last quarter," Megan said, slipping through the increasingly crowded halls.

"Why does that matter?" Darby asked.

"It's a short day. Classes will all be cut to about half an hour and squeezed into the first half of the day before lunch."

"You didn't tell me!" Darby said, relieved.

The shortened schedule was an incredible gift, she thought. Even if today was chaotic, they'd be able to get home and find Stormbird before dark.

"That's so cool," Darby said, crossing her fingers.

"Yeah, but"—Megan started to agree, then broke off to wave at someone who'd called her name— "even the slackers will be here turning in sick notes, so the office will be crowded. And you can't get started until we have your schedule."

Darby squared her shoulders, took longer strides, and looked straight ahead. Her last glance in the mirror had surprised her—no dark circles purpled the skin under her eyes from staying awake, fighting asthma. And her skin looked golden brown and smooth, more like her mother's than her own.

Of course, she was no beauty like her mother, but she'd changed a lot from the sickly girl who'd arrived at 'Iolani Ranch last month.

Darby took a deep breath, and realized that Lehua High smelled of flowers and greenery. Maybe palm trees, she thought, looking at the fronds swaying overhead. The only thing that reminded her of her school at home was the far-off scent of the sea.

And the office.

"Come on." Megan hooked her arm through Darby's and towed her inside.

It looked like every other school office Darby had ever been in: A counter barricaded students from the secretaries, desks, and computers.

Megan had been right. A long line of students led up to the counter.

When they claimed a place at the end of the line, Megan glanced at the office clock and moaned, "I'm going to be late to Spanish."

"Go ahead. This won't be hard," Darby said, but Megan shook her head no.

They'd stood waiting for about three minutes when Megan pivoted toward a girl with unruly red curls.

"Hey, girl!" Megan gave a good-natured shout so loud that everyone looked her way.

But Megan didn't notice.

"Hey, Meggie!" the redhead yelled back, and they high-fived each other.

*They must be on the soccer team together,* Darby thought.

"You lost the crutches!" Megan said.

"Yep." The other girl shifted her weight left, then knocked on her right knee. "No cast, bandages, nothing."

Darby's gaze darted away from the girl's red curls and freckles, past her knee, and focused on the faded blue-gray Western boots that almost matched her jeans.

"This is Ann, the one I told you about," Megan began, but just then the line moved up a few steps. When Ann limped to keep up with them, Megan asked, "So do you think you'll be playing again?"

"Don't even ask, or I'll cry," the girl said, though she didn't sound a bit teary. "My parents say three accidents and four surgeries in two years is enough. They won't sign for me to play soccer, or any other sport, until my growth plates are stabilized."

Megan looked confused, but Darby nodded and the other girls' eyes shifted to hers. And then they dropped to Darby's feet.

"Your boots rock," Ann said.

"Thanks," Darby answered. "So do yours."

"Oh, sorry," Megan said, "I don't know why I'm thinking of Spanish verb conjugations when you two need to meet each other. Ann Potter, this is my cousin, sort of, Darby Carter. Darby's from Los Angeles and Jonah's her grandfather."

Ann gave a thumbs-up sign.

"Darby, this is Ann Potter, the only eighth grader

in the history of Lehua High School to make the var-
sity soccer team, and you know what? She's from
Nevada, just like your horse!"

"No way!" Ann gasped. "You have a horse from
Nevada?"

"A mustang," Darby said, nodding, and she didn't
try to keep the pride from her voice.

"No way!" Ann repeated. "Where in Nevada?"

"War Drum Flats, in Darton County," Darby
recited. "It's kind of by—"

Ann grabbed her arm and shook it. She sure
didn't have the grip of a girl who'd just gotten off
crutches, but she didn't get to say whatever she'd
been about to, because a pleasant-faced woman wearing a Lehua High "staff" T-shirt was trying to get
their attention.

"Ladies?" she said, a bit impatiently.

Megan turned away from their conversation to
explain that Darby was a new student, but Darby
only heard the office lady say, "Her school records
arrived and she's ready to go," before Ann spoke up.

"I know exactly where War Drum Flats is. I used
to ride there. *We* had a ranch in Darton County!"
Ann's face turned thoughtful as studied Darby.
"Where did you live? It seems like we would have
been in school together."

"I didn't live there," Darby explained. "I was at
Dream Catcher Wild Horse Camp when BLM
brought my horse in."

"Dream Catcher what?"

"It's new," Darby told Ann. Then Darby's heart somersaulted in pride as she said, "My filly is a golden-red sorrel and her name's Hoku."

"Sweet," the other girl said with a sigh.

"Do you have horses here?" Darby asked.

"Oh, yeah," Megan put in, over her shoulder.

Darby wondered what it meant that Megan rolled her eyes.

"Ladies!" the office lady said, then laughed, "Oh, it's you, Ann. Perfect. Darby Carter's in your first class, so you can show her the way to Miss Day's room for English?"

Darby took the sheaf of papers the woman handed her. As the three girls left the office together, Darby felt relieved.

Now she knew two people at Lehua High, and her cousin would make three. Today might turn out okay.

"Since you've got everything under control, I'm sprinting to class. I might make it on time," Megan said.

"No problem," Ann answered.

Darby just smiled and looked down at her boots. Why did she feel shy when everything was working out fine?

"I'm not giving up on you, Crusher," Megan whispered to Ann, then she darted down the hall.

With a lopsided smile, Ann looked after her,

then turned to Darby.

"I'm an office aide," Ann said. "I give new students campus tours all the time, so here's what you need to know. . . ."

As they walked to class, Ann explained that Lehua High's buildings were arranged in an *H* shape. Grassy areas filled in the spaces on each end of the *H* and the bar in the middle was an actual bridge called the Link. Under it were the school office and library.

"If you ever feel like you're getting lost, go up on the Link." Ann pointed to the arch over the office and library buildings. "You'll have a view of the whole campus. The Link's where people meet before school, and at lunch and after school, too."

"You're good at this," Darby said.

Ann shrugged. "It's not like I always wanted to be an office aide, but after my last accident, they had to do something with me during my P.E. period."

Darby made a sympathetic sound and shortened her steps.

"You don't have to slow down for me," Ann snapped.

"Sorry," Darby said.

"No, *I'm* sorry." Ann shook her head. "I cracked my patella. My—"

"Kneecap," Darby filled in.

"Yeah, and it's improving every day, but I'm a little sensitive about this limp."

Darby searched for something to say, but Ann

wasn't the kind of girl who left a silence empty.

"I'm still a hellion on horseback," she whispered. "At least that's what my parents say."

Darby knew the word *hellion*. It only meant a mischievous person, but if she hadn't had such a good vocabulary, she might have thought it was something bad.

Darby laughed and said, "I'm just learning to ride."

"Really? And you adopted a mustang?" Ann looked surprised.

"She sort of adopted me," Darby said.

Ann shrugged and said, "Well, Jonah's the best teacher in the islands."

"In the country," Darby corrected, surprised at her own attempt at a joke.

"Just maybe in the world!" Ann teased. Then she held a finger in front of her lips to hush Darby's laughter, opened the door to a classroom, and said, "After you."

Chapter 5

"English, history, ecology, Sports P.E., Creative Writing, algebra," Ann read as she and Darby left their second class together.

Darby waited for Ann to look up so that she could ask her about her horses.

"Your schedule is just like mine, except that I have art instead of Creative—wait, are you an athlete?"

Darby's response was slow, because she'd just noticed the students around her weren't streaming toward their next classes.

"Not really," Darby said.

A few kids gathered in groups. Others sauntered across the green lawns, but most rushed toward metal carts that were quickly surrounded.

"But you have Sports P.E." Ann gestured at the schedule. "That's what I had, with Megan and the rest of the soccer team, and swim team, and—"

"Swim team? I used to be in Swim Club competitions at home," Darby said.

Her mother had filled out the school transfer paperwork before Darby had left home.

Darby wasn't sure if she was grateful or irritated that her mother had put her in Sports P.E., but she knew she was confused by all the idle students around her.

"What's going on?" Darby asked, her hand making a wide gesture.

"We have a fifteen-minute nutrition break," Ann said. "And our principal's serious about the nutrition part. We can only get fruit, nuts, and bento boxes. Plus juice or milk."

A boy who looked a lot like Harry Potter flagged Ann down, and though he talked with an animated voice and lots of hand motions, Darby didn't listen.

She slipped her hand into her jeans pocket. She'd decided to spend her lunch money on a bento box, just to learn what it was, when she spotted the Viking girl.

Darby had seen the word *stunning* used to describe people, but now she really understood it.

Metal-bright blond hair fell to shoulders that had to be six feet above the ground. Her sleeveless

Hawaiian print shift dress was slit up the sides to show muscular, tanned legs.

The astounding part, though, was that the Viking held milk cartons in each hand and chugged milk while other students—guys and girls—stood around her.

They clapped and chanted, "Go, go, go!"

"Is . . . ?" Darby attempted, unable to look away from the spectacle. "What . . . ?" she tried again.

Darby knew she was in trouble when sunlight winked on the Viking's silvery-black earrings and her head swiveled to take in Darby's interest.

*It's a cliché*, Darby told herself, but that didn't mean she could erase it from her mind. She'd never seen a girl more likely to knock her down and take her lunch money.

Somewhere a bell rang, and the students flowed back toward their classes again.

"Ecology is this way," Ann said. "Darby? Let's go. Now, since we don't have lunch today, I won't see you until algebra."

Darby followed her.

"Are you good at math?" Ann asked.

"I'm okay," Darby said. Then, holding her breath, she glanced over her shoulder.

The Viking was gone.

Darby knew she must have imagined the blonde's predatory stare.

Even if she hadn't, the girl had to be a junior or

senior. There was no way she'd have a class with an eighth grader like Darby.

The Viking stood outside the Lehua High gym. Towering over her friends, she held back her blond hair and leaned down to their eye level. Entertaining her followers with chatter about her black pearl earrings, the Viking didn't notice when Darby tripped.

Darby was quick enough to grab the doorjamb as she followed Megan into the locker room for P.E., her fourth-period class.

*Please don't let her be in this class,* Darby begged silently. *But she must be.*

"We got you a locker kind of close to ours." Megan punctuated her sentence with introductions to a dozen girls changing into gym clothes. "Coach let me," Megan added proudly.

Surrounded by Megan's soccer team, Darby slipped into her newly altered gym clothes.

She was starting to feel . . . not relaxed, but not paranoid, either—when Megan tugged at the hem of the red shorts Darby was wearing.

"My mom made those a little too short, didn't she?" Megan said as they emerged from the locker room into the sun.

Darby's heart was already pounding when she heard her name.

"Hi, Darby."

It took her a minute to recognize Miss Day. The

English teacher had exchanged her navy blue dress for a gym teacher's shorts, T-shirt, and clipboard.

"Hi, Miss Day," Darby said.

The teacher strolled on, as Megan elbowed Darby.

"Call her Coach, out here," Megan instructed. "She's the girls' soccer coach. And he," Megan muttered, "is Coach Roffmore."

Darby recognized the name from her schedule. She was pretty sure Roffmore was listed as her algebra teacher, too.

That was fine with her, Darby thought, because she had two fewer names to memorize.

She looked around, trying to figure out which girls played which sports.

"Roll call only today," Miss Day said.

"We get in alphabetical order," Megan explained, starting to move away from Darby.

"But I don't know anyone's last name. Tell me where to stand!"

"Okay," Megan said. She glanced down the front row of girls jostling into line. "There's your cousin."

Darby realized her hands had been clenched with tension until Megan said that. Standing beside her cousin would be better than standing beside a stranger.

At least that's what she thought until Megan's lips twisted a little, before she touched Darby's back and guided her to a place in front.

Darby was relieved when she saw she'd be facing Miss Day, until she realized Megan had steered her into the open space beside the Viking.

Oh, no. There had to be some mistake. Darby's head tilted back as she took in the girl's height and blondness. They couldn't possibly be related.

"Borden"—Megan addressed the big girl as one jock to another—"meet Carter. Your cousin."

Megan's jaw jutted forward as she waited for a response.

The Viking yawned. When her eyes reopened, they didn't settle on Darby, but on the male coach who'd just appeared before them.

"Coach Roffmore." Megan filled in the silence as Darby noticed a stocky man with a gray crew cut and legs corded with veins. "He's the swim coach."

Megan patted Darby on the back, then moved down the front line to her own spot, a few yards away.

"It's nice to meet you." Darby attempted to break the ice with her cousin, but the Viking said nothing and now that he was finished talking with Miss—no, *Coach* Day, Coach Roffmore fixed Darby with a stare.

*Does he want me to stop talking?* Darby wondered. *Is he blaming me for the extra paperwork that comes with being a new student?* Or did her inclusion in this gym class mean Coach Roffmore knew she could swim?

Swimming brought the white colt to mind. Kimo had called him a "sea horse," and Darby was smiling at that when the coach barked at her.

"Carter."

She nearly choked on her tongue before she managed, "Yes?"

"Since you've entered school so late in the year, the best way for you to get to know everyone is to call roll. Here."

As Coach Roffmore extended his clipboard toward her, Darby glanced at the girls around her. For the first time, she noticed how many were Hawaiian or Asian. How badly would she massacre the pronunciation of their names? And why would the coach do this to her?

Darby pictured herself falling to her knees with prayerful, upraised hands, begging the coach to reconsider, but Coach Roffmore didn't look like a man who'd back down.

Darby didn't remember her fingers ever sweating before, but her thumbs made faint prints on the roll sheet.

"Coretta?" Darby read in a shaky voice.

"Here."

"Use last names, then first. Carter, Darby," the coach demonstrated. When she nodded, he added, "Why don't you start from the end of the alphabet and work your way up to the front line, here."

"Okay," she said, then tried, "Yamaguchi, Gail?"

"Here."

"Waipunalei, Monica?" Darby stumbled over the

name, and wondered if you could die from humilia-
tion. But the girl corrected her good-naturedly.

Darby glanced up to thank her and noticed lots of
sympathetic eyes. Darby let out a bit of the breath
she'd been holding.

Even though the only part of Hawaiian that
Darby remembered was that the *e* sounds like an *a*,
there were enough names like Warren, Smith, and
Ota to keep her face from developing a permanent
blush.

*Almost done*, Darby thought.

"Kato, Megan," she called, and Megan winked at
her.

Cheryl Hong, a girl she'd met in the locker room,
actually flashed her a shaka sign.

By the time she reached her own name on the roll
sheet, Darby saw that the only two remaining names
were Borden and Ames. She could do this.

But then she spotted the Viking's impossible first
name.

*Duxelles*. It looked French, but *Borden* wasn't
French. Darby searched her memory. Borden was
Dutch, wasn't it? So that was like, German pronun-
ciation?

Great, that didn't help at all. Neither did the fact
that the letters swam before her eyes.

*Duxelles*.

She tried it in pieces, "Duck, ee —"

The girls burst into laughter. All but one.

Darby covered her mouth and shot a hopeless look at her cousin, but the reprimand came from behind her.

"Grow up, Carter. That was a lame joke," Coach Roffmore snapped.

Darby whirled to face him. The man's hands were on his hips and his eyes had narrowed.

Miss Day's expression said she knew it had been a mistake, but she looked past Darby to the lines of girls.

Darby kept hearing, "What did she say?" and "The new girl, did she just . . . ?" and the word *Duckie*, *Duckie*, *Duckie* jumped from the front row to the second, and waves of laughter built as the joke reached the last row.

Coach Roffmore blew a shrill tweet on his whistle and shouted, "All eyes on me!"

There was silence until Darby looked at the Borden girl and confessed, "I really don't know how to say your name. I'm sorry."

"Dew. Shell."

The two syllables quaked with outrage.

"Duxelles," Darby whispered, and this time she got it right.

 Chapter 6

$D$arby was counting the minutes until she could be around civilized creatures—horses, that is—again.

By her reckoning, she only had to last forty more minutes.

Creative Writing was going to be a fun class, but she'd come close to skipping it.

If responsibility to her teachers hadn't been so ingrained, she would have fled from P.E. to the office and begged for a schedule change.

She couldn't stand being in P.E. with Duxelles. Besides, she wasn't an athlete, and even though she liked having Megan in one of her classes, she'd rather miss that than be around Duxelles any more.

The big girl's *just you wait* sneer had unnerved

Darby in a way that none of the tough kids in Pacific Pinnacles ever had.

*Get a grip,* Darby told herself. She had to be over-reacting. They were *related*. If only for that reason, they'd have to get along.

Ann was already seated in algebra when Darby entered the classroom. And Darby would have bet Coach Roffmore didn't recognize her from P.E., except that he pointed out an empty desk in front of Ann for Darby to take.

"Great," Ann said, smiling. She sat sidesaddle at her desk, arranging her legs in a way that Darby guessed was easiest on her fractured patella. "How's it been going?"

"Okay," Darby said, and her spirits had just started rising again when Duxelles walked into class.

She was chugging milk again.

"Coach, I'm starving," said a muscular guy sitting up front. "Why can't *I* eat in class?"

"Borden's an athlete. She needs strong bones," the coach snapped.

"Yeah, she also needs to pass this class. It's her last try," Ann muttered to Darby. "And Marc? The hungry guy? He's a halfback. Not that he needs *his* calcium—"

"Potter!" the coach roared.

"Sorry, Coach. I didn't mean to moan," Ann said pitifully. "I can't seem to get in a comfortable position."

❊ ❊ ❊

A month before, when Darby had first arrived in Hawaii and Aunty Cathy had said that *she* was the school bus, Darby hadn't realized that she meant there was no real bus between Lehua High and the ranch.

Darby reached the school parking lot just as Kimo's faded maroon Ram Charger, with an 'Iolani Ranch owl painted on the door, pulled up next to the curb.

Aunty Cathy was driving instead of the Hawaiian cowboy. When Megan piled into the front seat, leaving Darby to clear a place in the cluttered backseat, she didn't mind.

"I hate to make you wait at school until Megan's done with soccer practice every day," Aunty Cathy said, sounding worried. "It's just lucky that practice was canceled today, but I can't make two round trips. . . ."

"It's okay," Darby assured her, because going to school tomorrow didn't matter.

All she wanted to do was saddle Navigator and ride out to find Stormbird today.

"Are you two going riding?" Aunty Cathy asked, making the right turn off the highway.

"Of course," Megan said. "You'll be a rich woman by sundown, Mom."

"It's a good thing, because Jonah could use a loan," she said, then hurried on, "I'm joking. Just be sure to get your chores done after you have lunch and before you go.

"And if I were you, I'd steer clear of Jonah. The bunkhouse water heater is still broken and Jonah's truck won't start. I guess he needs a new battery."

"Oh, that's why you're driving Kimo's truck," Megan said.

Her mother nodded.

The Ram Charger made its quiet way toward home, and when Darby glanced toward the rearview mirror, she caught Aunty Cathy's eyes watching her.

Darby waved and smiled.

Who cared about Coach Roffmore, the dreaded "Duckie," or even Jonah's broken-down truck? She was headed toward a world of horses.

Feeling recharged from lunch and the prospect of seeing Hoku, then meeting Megan to start their search at two o'clock, Darby ignored Aunty Cathy's warning to avoid Jonah and stopped next to her grandfather's truck.

All she saw of Jonah was his legs, sticking out from under the truck.

Darby scuffed her boots as she approached so that she wouldn't surprise him.

"Pick up your feet. You're going to wreck those boots," Jonah growled.

*Welcome home. How was your first day at school?*

Apparently Jonah was too cramped and uncomfortable to offer such greetings, but Darby just shook her head.

"I was being considerate," she told her grandfather. "I didn't want to sneak up on you."

She heard the clang of metal on metal, but nothing else for a full minute, so she asked, "How's your battery?"

"It's not the battery."

"Oh," Darby said.

She didn't know many car parts, so she stayed quiet, wondering if she should ask about the shocks. She'd always remembered the term because it struck her as a weird name for a piece of machinery.

Jonah began muttering, but Darby only picked out bits of sentences between the clanking of tools.

". . . land worth a million dollars an acre"—*clang*— "what I get for not"—*clank*—"selling it off . . ."

"Maybe I'll find the colt and win that money," Darby said.

"Do that."

"After all, I'm probably the only one to have seen Stormbird," she said, speaking down to Jonah's knees.

Jonah sighed, banged on the car's undercarriage, then said, "If you don't have anything else to do, check Hoku's fence. Judge has been leaning on it and no one's had time to reset the post, so you go see to it, yeah?"

"I will!"

Darby sprinted past the old fox cages toward her sorrel's corral.

Judge wasn't there, and the fence wasn't obviously sagging anyplace.

"Hoku!" she called to her horse, but the filly just stood in the middle of the corral, swishing her tail. "Are you bored, baby?"

Darby walked from post to post, pushing each one to see if it wobbled.

"I don't *really* know how you feel, because I wasn't born wild," she told her horse, "but I've been running around here, free, for an entire month. And even though I like school, the classrooms sure seem crowded compared to this."

Darby gestured toward the rolling green hills. When she turned back, Hoku gazed into her eyes with an understanding that startled Darby.

"You like the ranch and me just fine, but it's not the same as running free," she whispered. "But don't give up. As soon as I can ride you, we'll run and run and run until . . ." Darby glanced over her shoulder to make sure no one was listening. "I'll give you your head, isn't that what they call it?" Hoku shook, making a lion's mane of her long, flaxen hair. "Well, whatever it is, I'll be no trouble, snugged up there in your mane. I promise."

Darby worked her way around the corral twice, testing the fence posts. She refused to miss any weakness in them. She couldn't let Hoku escape, not when they were making brilliant progress together.

Darby shoved the posts with both arms, then turned around and leaned back with all of her weight. Not one of them budged.

Had Jonah just been trying to get rid of her?

Darby didn't know, but later she thought that it was probably a good thing she'd used up so much energy testing posts, calling in Jill and Peach, and helping Megan bridle Tango after she'd already tacked up Navigator, or she might have exploded when after they'd ridden for a few minutes Megan said, "Duxelles has a way of . . . well, she's kind of overwhelming, even if you've known her for a while."

Darby thought of the way Megan had set her jaw and glared at Duxelles as she'd said, *Borden, meet Carter.*

Navigator must have felt her tension, because he bolted a few steps toward the rain forest and Darby spent a few minutes gathering her reins and reassuring the brown gelding before she asked, "Does she bother *you*?"

"Not since my growth spurt," Megan said, "but she used to trip me in fifth grade."

"My cousin," Darby repeated as they passed the barely visible path to the old plantation. "She doesn't look . . . you know . . ."

Darby didn't say Duxelles didn't look Hawaiian, because she'd learned almost immediately that Hawaiians came in all shapes and colors. Instead, she gestured toward her hair.

"Blame White Water Willy, I guess," Megan had said. "Yawn and Duxelles look like him."

Darby nodded, then asked, "What's up with a boy named Yawn?"

"It's Dutch," Megan said, shrugging. "*J-A-N*, you know?"

"Oh," Darby said.

Suddenly both dogs froze. The smaller black dog, Jill, could have been Peach's shadow.

Both horses stopped, too. Darby noticed Tango looking toward the rain forest instead of the trail to Night Digger Point Beach.

"Up here," Megan said. She clucked at Tango and touched her heels to the rose roan, urging her up a rise of ground.

Offshore, they saw two white plumes of water and heard a sound Darby didn't recognize.

Megan did, though.

"Jet Skis," she said. "They're probably people from Sugar Sands Cove, but they usually don't get around this far."

"I bet they're looking for Stormbird," Darby said.

"But you have to be rich to stay at Sugar Sands Cove," Megan said.

Darby shrugged. Who would turn down the fun of a treasure hunt or the reward at the end of it, even if they already had plenty of money?

"Well, forget them! We'll pick up the pace and

find him first," Megan insisted. "And here's how."

Darby was surprised by Megan's thorough knowledge of the ocean. Megan explained that a strong coastal current ran from Night Digger Point Beach to Message Bottle Landing.

"That's why they call it that," Megan pointed out. "If you throw a bottle into the waves off Night Digger, it will end up at Message Bottle Landing."

"And if a person jumps in?" Darby asked, thinking how hard she and Hoku had fought against the waves after they'd swum out from Crescent Cove.

"Same thing for a person or a horse. Especially a little lightweight colt!"

"Wow," Darby said. She glanced toward the roaring Jet Skis. It was pretty unlikely that those people knew half as much as Megan did.

"I'll take Jill with me," Megan said, "and you keep Peach, yeah? I'll ride up the shore toward Message Bottle and you go to Night Digger."

Darby's hands began shaking. She couldn't help it, even though she knew she was being silly.

The reason Jonah had ordered them to take the dogs was that Aunt Babe had encouraged Manny to search for the valuable cremello colt.

"I know what you're thinking," Megan said, but then she began counting their safety precautions on her fingers. "We'll each have a dog, I'm riding twice as far as you'll have to—"

Darby opened her mouth to protest because she

didn't want either of them to come face-to-face with Manny.

"—and Manny is afraid of Jonah."

Darby knew greed outweighed fear for lots of people, but Megan was already turning her horse, promising she'd hurry back.

"What if you find Stormbird?" Darby said. "You can't hurry back with him."

"Unless . . ." Megan drew the word out, and Darby was pretty sure the older girl was stalling. "If I find Stormbird, I'll, uh . . ."

Megan glanced at each side of her saddle.

"You don't have a rope," Darby pointed out. "Neither of us has a belt. Or shoelaces, so you can't lead him back home."

"He's probably not old enough to know how to lead, anyway," Megan said, frowning as she smoothed her hand over her mare's black mane.

Tango was what Jonah called "green-broke." She could be ridden and she understood most of Megan's signals, but Darby doubted the rose roan would tolerate something like Megan wrestling a colt up over her back, let alone agreeing to carry it all the way back to the ranch.

*We didn't think this out very well.* Darby didn't say it out loud, because all the excitement was her fault. She was the one who'd seen Stormbird. She'd claimed she knew approximately where he was. And she'd just sort of pictured the colt following

Navigator home like he'd started to last night.

"I'm dumber than I thought." Darby looked down at her saddle horn.

When Megan chuckled, Darby looked up. Her remark hadn't been that funny.

"Maybe *you* are, but I'm not," Megan teased, and Tango must have sensed her rider's excitement, because the rose roan's legs pranced in place and she tossed her black mane.

"You're going to love this!" Megan assured Darby.

As she waited, Darby smiled, even though she had no idea what was coming next.

Chapter 7

"Pretend you're riding away from me," Megan told Darby.

"Why?"

"Just do it. Turn Navigator down that path like you're riding to Tutu's."

Darby's thoughts darted around impatiently as she turned Navigator away from Megan and Tango.

Then Megan whistled.

Darby looked back, but the summons wasn't for her.

With lifted ears, Jill and Peach stared at Megan.

She swung her arm toward the departing Navigator.

"Walk up," she ordered, and the dogs followed

the brown gelding until she added, "Away to me."

The dogs trotted alongside Navigator, then crossed in front of him.

The big gelding jerked his head up in annoyance. Before Darby moved the reins, Navigator turned away from the dogs.

The Quarter Horse outweighed the dogs by hundreds of pounds. He had heavy hooves and hard muscles and could have trotted right over them, but he didn't. He moved back to Megan because the dogs told him to.

"Wow!" Darby shook her head in amazement.

"And a little colt will be easy for them," Megan said.

Megan and Darby stopped where the foliage was sparse and a trail led to Tutu's cottage.

"Now we just have to find him," Darby said, and she was smiling, even as she rode on alone.

"Let's go, boy," Darby said.

Navigator took long strides, forcing Peach to bound along beside him. In just a minute or two, the sound of Tango's hooves, moving away, was covered by sighing waves.

Darby rode the same path she had yesterday, before her first day of school, and pushed aside the thought that the Viking was her cousin.

"It doesn't mean we have to be friends," she muttered to Navigator.

As soon as sand began muffling the plop of Navigator's hooves, she slowed him to a walk and scanned the beach for the colt.

This was the spot where she'd first seen him. Nearby was the truck-sized rock with the tide pool on top, which still overflowed with salty bubbles.

Darby was looking past it to the ocean when Peach began growling.

"Shh," Darby said, concentrating on something white that was bobbing on the waves. It didn't look like foam or a gull.

Navigator dropped his head and looked back at Peach.

The dog crouched, fur rising on his back, glaring at the empty path behind them.

Chills covered Darby's arms. *Chicken skin.* She tried to joke with herself by recalling the expression Kimo used for goose bumps, but Peach wasn't joking.

What did he hear? Or see? Compared to the dog, she was deaf and blind, but instinct told Darby she was being watched.

Not by the rabid pig, Darby told herself as she remembered the dangerous animal that she and Hoku had encountered in the rain forest. The pig was dead.

Not Black Lava, either. Though they were near Crimson Vale, Darby doubted the wild stallion would provoke this reaction from Peach.

Jonah had trained the dogs to handle stock gently.

To Peach, wouldn't Black Lava count as stock?

A breeze wandered through the ohia trees.

Darby stared at the forest for so long, she had to remind herself of her goal—the colt. She hadn't seen him in the forest, but rather along the shore.

Darby swiveled in the saddle. The patch of white she'd glimpsed before had vanished. She was alone with the black sand and quiet waves.

A whine made her look down at Peach. The dog had taken a few steps and looked back at her for permission.

"Alone, but I have Peach," she said. The dog answered with a tail wag. "And Navigator, my fine horse."

She stroked the gelding's glossy neck.

"I'm just scaring myself silly," she told the horse, but she couldn't help remembering how Jonah had lectured her about letting Hoku keep her wild instincts.

Maybe, Darby thought, her own instincts, and not her imagination, were scaring her. What then? Should she listen to them?

Birds rose in a cloud of color and cries above the treetops.

"We're out of here," Darby told Navigator. "What good's the money if I'm not around to use it?"

She rode at a lope to find Megan, and Peach bounded beside the horse, openmouthed and watchful.

❊ ❊ ❊

Megan hadn't seen the colt. She hadn't picked up signs of Manny, or anything else dangerous, and though she told Darby she'd done the right thing by riding away from Night Digger Point Beach, Megan acted scornful, not scared of Cade's stepfather.

"He's such a jerk," Megan said.

For a few seconds the girls watched the dogs come together in a tumbling greeting, as if they'd been apart for weeks.

Then, Megan said, "I used to have nightmares that he killed my dad."

"Megan," Darby said, wincing for her friend.

"I mean, I was there, and I saw the accident. I know what happened to my dad, but really? I think Manny has a thing about scaring people. He wants them to see him as a movie villain, slinking through the woods all silent and scary."

"It works on me," Darby said, even as another worry tried to shove its way from the back of her mind to the front. She ignored it to listen to Megan.

"Think of Jonah and Cade, and my mom, and Kimo and Kit—" Megan broke off, shaking her head. "They're all on our side, all standing behind us. And what does he have? Dee."

"Cade's mom?" Darby asked.

"My mom calls Dee a 'sorry excuse for a mother.'"

"I'm probably paranoid from growing up in the city," Darby offered, but then a nagging thought emerged. "Why would Aunt Babe encourage Manny to find Stormbird?"

Megan took off her baseball cap, then put it back on, slightly repositioned, before she shrugged and said, "He would have seen it on TV, anyway, and that was the best way to get lots of people searching, or—" Megan stopped and shot a cautious glance at Darby. "I don't know Babe that well, but you know some people say the end justifies the means."

The end would be getting Stormbird back, Darby thought. The means could be Manny.

"So, speaking of Babe, how are we going to get that reward money?" Megan reminded Darby.

Riding back to the ranch, they brainstormed ideas for how to catch Stormbird.

"That's the best one, so far," Darby said of Megan's suggestion that they bring a nursing mare— without her foal—down to the beach.

"It could backfire. She could kick at him, or nip," Megan mused. "But he'd be close enough, by the time the mare refused him, that the dogs could herd him home."

Darby tried to concentrate. She mentally walked herself through the strategy for tomorrow, but she couldn't stop replaying Jonah's voice, repeating Aunt Babe's opinion of Manny.

*He's violent. I don't like that about him, but he knows this island. . . .*

Darby was glad Megan was as determined as she was to capture Stormbird. Going after the colt alone just wouldn't be smart.

Chapter 8

The dogs, Jill and Peach, bounded ahead of the horses. With sharp barks they circled the brown Land Rover, letting Darby and Megan know that Jonah was still working under the truck.

Bart, the young Aussie, raced up to the older dogs. He made play bows and whined to be included in their game.

Megan whistled as she rode Tango toward the tack shed. Jill and Bart followed her, but Darby was left to discipline Peach.

"Peach, no! Come back here."

She didn't have much luck, since the orange-and-white dog had already flopped on his belly, noticed the spot where his master's jeans had pulled up above his boots, and begun licking Jonah's leg.

*I bet that tickles*, Darby thought. She tried not to laugh as Jonah's leg jiggled to escape Peach's tongue.

Then Sass trotted up, turned his blue merle head sideways, and made an up-and-down begging sound. Darby thought Sass was asking if he could join Jonah under the truck.

"Go away," came her grandfather's voice. "I hate dogs."

Of course he didn't, Darby thought, smiling. From her saddle she had a great view of the comedy between her grandfather and the dogs.

"I can see your horse's hooves," Jonah said. He sounded tired and annoyed. "Unless you and Navigator want to crawl under and fix this beast, do something with those dogs."

Peach and Sass must have heard their master's exasperation. When Darby smooched to the dogs, they abandoned Jonah and trotted on each side of Navigator as she rode to the tack shed.

Megan had already put up Tango and returned to Sun House by the time Darby unbridled her dark brown gelding, then haltered and tied him to a ring on the wooden wall.

As her hands worked on Navigator, she hummed and thought about her homework. Even though she'd miss her long weekday hours with Hoku, there was a comfort in being back in a routine. Both her English and Creative Writing teachers wanted writing samples from her by tomorrow and she was pretty sure she could do a decent job for them.

Aunty Cathy's voice disrupted Darby's thoughts, but Megan's mother was talking to Jonah.

She came from the house holding the telephone, then squatted next to the truck.

"It must be pretty important," Darby told Navigator.

After all, Aunty Cathy had been the one to tell her and Megan they should avoid Jonah.

Still watching the two adults, Darby eased back the leather from the buckle's tongue and released Navigator's cinch.

Darby stood on tiptoe, grabbed the saddle front and back, and hauled it off. The saddle blankets came with it and dropped over her boots. Darby tripped, but didn't fall.

She lost track of her grandfather and Cathy as she remembered how she'd almost fallen earlier today, going into the Lehua High gym.

"I don't like being clumsy," she whispered to Navigator.

Maybe she was still learning to walk in boots, Darby thought, looking down at the scuffed reddish pair she'd decided to wear for chores.

She wanted to keep her new boots clean and smooth.

For a few seconds, Darby weighed the possibility of not wearing her boots to school tomorrow. Most everyone wore slippers—what she'd called flip-flops back in California—or sneakers.

Then, thinking of Ann, Darby felt stubborn. In a good way.

Darby loved her new boots, and since they were part of who she was in Hawaii, she was absolutely going to wear them whenever she felt like it.

"And I'll get used to walking in them," Darby said, brushing the sweat marks from Navigator's black-coffee coat.

When she'd finished, she realized Aunty Cathy was still beside the truck.

Curiosity may have killed the cat, but Darby couldn't not investigate. She approached on tiptoe, but Aunty Cathy noticed her.

As Aunty Cathy pushed her messy brown-blond hair away from her eyes, Darby realized that Jonah must still be on the phone, under the truck.

Cathy held her index finger against her lips in a shushing motion before she mouthed the name, *Babe.*

Darby was surprised, but she was pretty sure she hadn't made a sound when Jonah yelled, "What!"

It sounded as if he sat up, or tried to, and hit his head on the underside of the truck.

Darby winced.

Aunty Cathy stood. She made a "he's all yours" gesture and rushed away, but Peach took her place next to Darby for just seconds before he crawled under the car and Darby heard him licking her grandfather again.

"Not my neck," Jonah moaned. "Can't you just let me die in peace?"

Darby smothered her giggle, but Jonah shouted, "I'm talking to you!"

"Me?"

In response, Jonah threw the phone out from under the truck.

"Put that in the trough, will you?"

Guessing that she'd misunderstood, Darby leaned over and peered under the truck.

"What?" she asked her grandfather.

The space in which he was wedged looked tight and dark as a coffin.

"What happened to you?" he yelled.

"Me? Nothing."

"You didn't hear when I told you to throw that blasted phone in the horses' trough."

Darby walked away, but she decided to carry the phone back into the house instead of following Jonah's orders.

She struggled out of her boots and headed to the kitchen, where Aunty Cathy waited with raised eyebrows.

Darby hung up the phone.

"He told me to throw it into the horse trough."

"When he's talking to Babe, he's not always . . ." Aunty Cathy hesitated.

"Rational?" Darby suggested.

"Levelheaded," Cathy substituted.

Just then, Jonah came into the house. He shucked off his boots. Clothes dirty and hands greasy, he frowned at them.

*No one likes to be gossiped about,* Darby thought. *Not even a grandfather.*

Still, when Aunty Cathy spoke, she didn't sound apologetic.

"I know going along with one of Babe's ideas grates on your nerves."

"Down to the bone," Jonah agreed.

"Even if it is a *good* idea."

"It's not. Think of the cost."

"She'd pay for guest insurance and provide their transportation over here," Cathy persisted.

"I don't raise dude horses."

"It's something to think about," Aunty Cathy said. She took a clean apron from a drawer and shook it out. Putting it on, she faced away from them, and Darby thought the conversation was finished.

But Jonah wasn't satisfied with the end of their discussion.

"Do you think Kit came all the way from Nevada and signed on to be a dude wrangler?" Jonah asked. "And what about Cade? That boy's set his heart on being a paniolo."

For a full minute, Aunty Cathy didn't turn around. Her hands appeared behind her back and tied her apron strings with a definite jerk. But that was the only sign she showed of irritation until she faced Jonah.

"Did I sign on to do this?" She gestured at the kitchen. "No, I was just a paniolo's wife who kept your ranch accounts for a little extra money. But I don't want to move to Honolulu or return to the mainland so I can be a travel agent again. I don't want that life for Megan or—" Cathy stopped and took a breath.

"Jonah, I love this ranch—just like Cade and Kit do. I'm willing to do what it takes to keep it afloat, and I bet they are, too."

*Me too,* Darby thought, but this was no time to chime in. This discussion, or argument, or whatever it was had all kinds of undercurrents she didn't understand. She wasn't going to help by getting involved, so she backed out of the kitchen.

Neither Cathy nor Jonah noticed her leave, and though Darby meant to go to her room and start her homework, she went outside instead.

Darby turned the corner of Sun House and climbed the white iron staircase that reminded her of a city fire escape because it rose up the outside wall of the house to the apartment above.

Pip, the Katos' dandelion puff of a dog, yapped at the approach of company. Megan had already scooped up her dog and opened the door when Darby reached the top step.

"Hi," Darby said. She leaned over to look into Pip's

shaggy face and a rose-petal tongue licked her nose.

"Come in," Megan said, gesturing with the dog before she set Pip down and closed the screen door.

Megan must have been doing homework. A yellow pencil had been poked through her thick cherry Coke–colored hair, and a clutter of textbooks and notebooks shared the white wicker couch with Pip and a pile of tropical print pillows.

"Are they fighting?" Megan asked, pointing to the floor of the apartment.

"Not exactly," Darby said. "Or if they are, it's not the kind of fighting I recognize."

Darby tried to explain what she'd heard of Babe's suggestion. Megan brushed her words aside.

"Don't even try to figure it out," Megan said as she poured them both some sun tea. "It's not worth it."

Every time Darby came into the upstairs apartment, she loved it. Perched atop Sun House, it felt like a tree house.

Vintage ukuleles hung on one wall and their polished wood made them look like art. Hula dolls positioned on a shelf between flowerpots danced in a breeze that played music from wind chimes.

Darby didn't look at the desk in the corner. It held some things of her mother's. She wanted to look through them for clues to the battle with Jonah that had kept her mother from returning to her Hawaiian home.

Wouldn't that be an invasion of her mother's privacy? Not if she asked permission, but Darby didn't have the nerve to do that.

*Until you do,* she lectured herself, *you'll just have to live with the curiosity.*

"Hold these," Megan said, and once Darby held both glasses of iced tea, Megan shoved her schoolwork to the floor, clearing room for them both to sit on the couch.

"I've been thinking about our plan to catch the colt," Megan said when they were settled. "I've come up with an idea, and we just can't wait."

"Okay," Darby said.

"Do you know Kimo and Cade are out riding the ranch borders right now, keeping weird people from wandering onto Jonah's property?"

"Already?" Darby asked.

"One guy Kimo ran across this morning was sitting in your little rain-forest shelter with a stun gun," Megan said, and Darby gasped.

"You're right," Darby said. "Even if we didn't want the money—"

"Which we do," Megan put in.

"Sure, but we've got to keep that little colt safe." Darby leaned against the back of the couch. She closed her eyes, thinking. "You have practice from two thirty until four, right? And since your mom doesn't want to drive back and forth—and I don't blame her—I'm stuck there until four, too, and . . ."

"Do you remember the part where I said I had a

plan?" Megan asked, then took a long sip of her drink.

"What is it?"

"When we get home, it will be about five o'clock—"

"And it will be dark by seven, so that doesn't give us much time, and Jonah—" Darby broke off when she saw Megan staring at her over the brim of her glass. "I just can't get in trouble again. What if he sends me home to my dad? He could do that, you know."

*"Please."* Megan's tone implied she was insulted.

"Sorry," Darby apologized. "Go ahead."

"So, even though we'll get a late start, we'll bring a snack with us, and a nursing mare, and good old Owl Eyes."

Totally bewildered, Darby reviewed her memories for the last month, trying to remember who Megan meant.

"It means we'll have to split the money three ways," Megan said.

Darby nodded, then waited for the puzzle pieces of information to fit together, but they refused.

At last, Darby had to ask, "Who or what is good old Owl Eyes?"

Chapter 9

"Cade, of course."

"Ohhh." Darby drew the word out in under-standing, because the nickname Owl Eyes made sense when Megan applied it to the young paniolo.

At first, Darby had thought Cade's reputation for being able to see in the dark had to be an exaggeration. But she'd reassessed her opinion last week.

Unlike her Southern California home, where stores, parking lots, athletic fields, and condominiums were illuminated by searchlights, neon, and incandescent lamps, Wild Horse Island had almost no outdoor lights.

When the sun went down, it got *dark*. And midnight in the rain forest was even darker, since the canopy blocked out the starshine and moonlight, too.

And yet Cade had seen a suffering boar in that blackness, and killed it with a single, merciful shot.

Looking at Megan's impatient expression, Darby asked, "You think Jonah and your mom will let us stay out after dark looking for Stormbird if Cade comes with us?"

"Yes." Megan sounded disgusted but sure. "It's not fair, but yes. Just let me handle it."

Cade was good with horses, too, Darby thought. Only Hoku didn't like him, and that was not Cade's fault.

Darby's wild filly didn't like any men.

Since Cade could see in the dark and handle horses, and would probably be willing to help them search the island's southern shore, why did Megan's idea make her uneasy?

Darby couldn't come up with any answer better than selfishness.

When she'd first set eyes on Stormbird, she'd thought, *Don't let him belong to anyone else.*

"It's too bad we'll have to divvy up the money," Megan said, misinterpreting Darby's silence, "but one third of something is better than half of nothing, right?"

"Absolutely! It's a good idea," Darby said, and she didn't have to explain further, because Aunty Cathy called them to dinner.

"Come on, girls. Don't let your fish tacos get soggy."

"Fish tacos?" Darby considered herself an adventurous eater, but she felt a bit doubtful.

"They're great," Megan promised on her way out the apartment door. "Mom fries mahimahi, then makes this fruit salsa. It's not spicy. It has mangos and papaya chopped up, and lime squeezed over it or something. Yum."

Megan rolled her eyes in anticipation, then hurried down the stairs with Darby on her heels.

But then Darby realized what bothered her about Megan's plan, and she stopped.

"You don't suppose," Darby said, trying to sound casual when Megan looked back, "that Cade's whole seeing-in-the-dark thing is hereditary, do you?"

Darby's memory replayed Manny, stepping silently onto the path in front of her, Cade, and Megan as they'd ridden out of Crimson Vale a couple of weeks ago.

Through three long heartbeats, Darby waited, but then Megan gave an understanding smile.

"Manny is Cade's *step*father, remember?"

Darby gave a self-deprecating moan. "Sure I do. Now."

How could she have forgotten? Cade and Manny weren't related by blood. Of course they couldn't both see in the dark.

Darby felt so relieved, she wasn't even embarrassed. She hurried down the white iron steps and caught up with Megan.

Suddenly, fish tacos sounded like they might be worth a try.

Neither Megan nor Aunty Cathy mentioned the swelling over Jonah's eye, and since Darby was pretty sure he'd struck his forehead on the underside of the truck when he'd been talking with Babe on the telephone, she didn't, either.

He'd been so angered by his sister's proposal that 'Iolani Ranch host tourist rides, Jonah had forgotten where he was.

So Darby was surprised when Cathy brought the subject up all over again.

"What if we only had guest rides two or three days a week?" Aunty Cathy suggested. "Maybe just on weekends?"

"I'm shorthanded as it is," Jonah said.

"Guest rides?" Megan paused with a taco halfway to her mouth.

"My sister plans to level her stable and replace it with a 'state-of-the-art' gym. . . ."

"I'm pretty sure that's Phillipe's idea," Aunty Cathy put in, referring to Babe's polo-player husband.

"And have me babysit her guests who want to ride," Jonah finished.

Megan leaned back in her chair. She'd only mulled over the idea for a few seconds when she observed, "Some of those riders would probably be cool guys."

Aunty Cathy sighed, Darby blushed, and Jonah said, "See? Is that what you want?"

"I was joking," Megan told them all, but Darby still wished Megan hadn't said that.

Darby took a bite of rice, taco, and fruit salsa, then started over again with robotic slowness.

Part of her wanted the ranch to stay exactly as it was now. But Jonah worried about money a lot.

And now, if she supported the idea of the ranch earning extra funds with tourist rides, Jonah might believe she was thinking the same thing as Megan.

"Mom has a background in tourism," Megan told Jonah. "She'd make things run right. She wouldn't let it be tacky."

"Thanks, honey," Aunty Cathy said, and when Jonah didn't respond to Megan's support, Aunty Cathy added, "He knows, but we'll talk about it later."

"She offered me her cremellos," Jonah said. "She says they'd make the start of a good dude string. What makes her think I want those watery-eyed weaklings on the place?"

Darby shook her head in disbelief. The colt she'd seen hadn't been a weakling. Sure-footed over lava spikes and daredevilish with Navigator, he seemed at home in this wild and varied country.

And Flight, the colt's mother, had looked lean and muscular on TV—a beautiful horse, but one that earned her feed, Darby thought. Even as the words flowed through her mind, she realized how much her ideas about horses had changed since she'd come to the ranch.

Darby promised herself she'd correct Jonah's impressions of cremellos later, but she'd just realized she could change the subject to something no one would fight over.

"So, I had my first day of Hawaiian school," Darby announced.

Smile lines crinkled around Jonah's eyes.

"And what did you think, Granddaughter?"

"It was great," Darby said. "I'm not behind or ahead of my mainland classes. I'm pretty sure I'll do okay on my homework. Tonight's, anyway."

"Of course, Duxelles was a jerk to her."

*Megan!* Darby yelled silently.

"What kind of jerk?" Aunty Cathy asked, but her daughter had already caught Darby's wide-eyed stare.

"You know," Megan said vaguely. "Just a jerk."

Jonah and Aunty Cathy turned to Darby. She couldn't let them think she'd made an enemy of her cousin already.

"I had to call roll in P.E. and I mispronounced her name," Darby said.

"Not Borden," Megan said, then sucked in a breath and only went on to say, "Sorry."

Darby tried not to sound silly as she added, "I have the same teacher for P.E. and English. Her name is Miss Day, and—"

"Your cousin is one big strapping girl," Jonah observed.

"You make her sound like a horse," Cathy scolded.

"No offense to horses," Megan put in.

"Megan! Duxelles is . . ." Aunty Cathy hesitated, tucking her blond-brown hair behind her ears. "Well, she's . . ."

Jonah chewed meditatively, swallowed, then nodded at Darby and said, "You'll take care of yourself."

"Yep," Darby assured him, though it was possible Jonah's confidence in her was undeserved.

"Just remember," her grandfather said, pointing the tines of his fork at her, *the smallest flea can make a big body squirm.*"

Instantly a grin claimed Darby's face.

"Is that a Hawaiian proverb?"

"Just an old saying," Jonah answered.

"I love it," Darby said.

She wasn't tiny, but she'd always been kind of frail, and the image of a feisty flea making the Viking girl dance with discomfort delighted Darby.

Still smiling, Darby glanced at Aunty Cathy for her reaction and discovered she still looked thoughtful, searching for something nice to say about Duxelles.

Darby folded her napkin and set it on the table.

The sooner she finished her homework, the sooner she could go to bed. The sooner she got to school in the morning, the sooner she could catch Stormbird!

Still, she wondered: Was it significant that even Aunty Cathy couldn't think of one nice thing to say about Duxelles Borden?

Darby was almost asleep when the kitchen phone rang.

Megan and Aunty Cathy were in their upstairs apartment. Jonah was in his library under the stairs.

A glance at her bedside clock told Darby it was ten o'clock. Not the middle of the night, she thought, but what if it was her mother?

She heard Jonah muttering as he climbed out of his hideaway and into the living room. Then Darby caught the sounds of his feet padding into the kitchen.

The phone was still ringing.

"Yeah," he said, leaving no question it was too late to be calling.

In the quiet, Darby heard a floorboard creak overhead.

Jonah wouldn't make her wait until tomorrow to find out what her mother had to say, would he?

"Yeah," Jonah repeated. "I'll get him."

The front door opened and Jonah left.

*Him,* Darby's thoughts raced. Kimo was gone, so

the call must be for Cade or Kit. If it was news for Kit, it was coming in the middle of the Nevada night. That couldn't be good.

Outside, one of the dogs gave a sound that was half bark, half howl.

It seemed like forever before footsteps returned.

Darby strained her ears to listen.

"I'm going to bed." Jonah's voice boomed through the quiet house, but his last words were harder to hear. "Take your time."

Jonah's footsteps paused outside Darby's room. She didn't move a finger or toe. He kept walking.

Finally she heard Cade's voice.

"Mom?"

There was something so childish in his voice, it hurt Darby to hear it.

But the gentle tone vanished after he'd listened for a minute or so.

"Yeah," he snapped. "Yeah, I know." Cade's tone had turned surly. Was he still talking to his mother?

"Why should I ever put *any* horse in your hands again? Let alone a foal." Cade fell silent and didn't speak for what seemed like a long time.

"You don't scare me," he said finally, but after he slammed the phone down, he said something softly. It sounded like, "Aw, no," but Darby wasn't even sure the words were English.

Cade's boots strode partway down the hall toward Jonah's room, then stopped.

He turned back toward the front door and stopped again.

Darby was about to go ask Cade if he needed her help, when there was a fleshy sound, as if Cade had punched his fist into his other palm.

Darby heard nothing else until the door closed softly behind him. Through her window came the sound of boots crossing the ranch yard.

Had Cade's mother asked him to bring her Stormbird?

The more Darby tried to make sense of the half-conversation, Cade's anger, and his hesitation in going to Jonah for help, the more confused she felt.

Chapter 10

In her rush to get ready for school the next morning, Darby forgot about Cade's phone call.

*Why did I spend so much time feeding Hoku and playing with Francie?* Darby asked herself as she brushed hay off her light blue shirt, then pulled her hair into her usual ponytail.

She only remembered Cade's late-night caller and his words about a foal when she and Megan stood fidgeting in front of Sun House, waiting for Kimo to show up and drive them to school.

"He's always late," Megan grumbled. "We would have a better chance of being on time if we saddled up and rode to school."

Since Jonah's truck was out of commission, they

had no other choice, but both girls stared at the road as if concentration would make the maroon truck materialize.

"What if we walk out to the highway?" Darby asked. "Or at least as far as the gate?"

"Good idea," Megan said. "From the cattle guard gate to here is half a mile. I used to jog it."

Together they settled their backpacks more firmly on their shoulders and began walking.

"At least I took care of our search party problem," Megan told Darby when they were about halfway to the street.

"You did?"

"Yeah, I talked to Mom last night and she said she'd handle Jonah, but—didn't you hear me talking to Cade?"

Darby shook her head, but Cade's voice saying *Mom?* and *You don't scare me* came back to her.

Cade had been talking with his mother, and they'd fought. But it hadn't been a normal parent-kid spat. It sounded like an old, cold fight, and it had involved horses.

"Don't frown," Megan said. "Cade said he'd go with us the minute we got home. He seemed . . ."

"What?" Darby demanded.

"Usually he's so laid-back, but he actually seemed eager to go tonight," Megan said. And then she shrugged, but Darby wondered if Cade wanted to catch the colt before his parents did.

\* \* \*

Darby checked the room number for her English class, caught the door before it closed, and slipped inside. She glanced around for her desk, saw Ann pointing to it, and managed to take her seat a minute before the tardy bell.

Ann gave her a thumbs-up as Miss Day entered the room.

Darby fanned her face with one hand while she dug for her homework with the other.

Racing in that close to the bell was embarrassing. She didn't want her teacher to think she was always behind.

But Miss Day seemed pleased when Darby turned in her writing sample. And later, Darby managed to make a good point in history class when her teacher called on her.

She didn't even stare when her cousin repeated yesterday's milk-chugging exhibition during Nutrition Break, because she and Ann were talking about horses.

"We train therapy horses," Ann was explaining.

Darby heard a note of pride in the girl's voice that hadn't been there when they talked about soccer or school.

"For kids with disabilities, or personal problems?" Darby asked, thinking of the HARP program Sam Forster had told her about.

"Kids or adults who need horses," Ann said. "We

keep it vague on purpose so we just have to be picky about the horses, not people who get them. We mostly use rescue horses—any age, any breed—with 'kind eyes.' That's how my parents decide whether to take them in."

"Is that what you guys did in Nevada, too?" Darby asked.

She couldn't think of a much better profession than helping horses and people at the same time.

"No, we raised cattle—*went broke* raising cattle, according to my dad. It was half my grandpa's ranch. *He* made the mistake of selling Shan Stonecrow a horse, too," Ann reminded Darby of Hoku's last owner. "Anyway, when we left Nevada, my parents were so burned out, they thought they'd never want another ranch.

"But being full-time tourists didn't last long, and with the money they got from our old place—which Toby, my little brother, and I didn't approve of selling, by the way—they bought a house and a little spread and we started training horses."

"That is so cool," Darby said.

The rest of the morning went smoothly, and Darby felt satisfied with her second day of school. At first.

It was only when she was on her way to P.E., without Ann, that Darby realized she'd somehow ended up trailing behind her cousin and her friends, just like she had yesterday.

Darby hung back, hoping for invisibility.

When they reached P.E., she'd have to stand right beside the big girl, again.

Darby told herself not to be intimidated. If she really was the feisty flea that could make a big body squirm, she'd use yesterday's roll call mistake and call her cousin not *Dew shell*, but Duckie.

She dropped back a few steps, resolving to do just that, but only in the privacy of her mind.

Darby's determination to remain unnoticed worked until she heard a word she couldn't ignore.

"All Babe cares about is finding that *horse*," Duckie scoffed.

Stormbird! Her cousin must be talking about the lost white colt.

Darby closed the space between them with a few long steps.

"She should never have offered a reward," Duckie went on. "I mean, all these strange people are calling and showing up like bats out of a belfry."

It took Darby a second to realize what her cousin meant. Wasn't the expression, *Bats* in *your belfry*? Meaning you were crazy?

She shrugged to herself. So what if Duckie got the phrase wrong? Darby decided she couldn't very well blame Duckie for that, when she often did something similar. She sometimes mispronounced words that she'd read but never heard.

And now one of the girls walking ahead was

asking about Yawn. *Jan,* Darby corrected herself.

It wasn't easy to tell from the back, but Darby thought she remembered calling that girl's name yesterday. *Selena.* Darby thought it was because the girl appeared as dark and sleek as a seal.

"I'd love it if we could all hang around together. . . ."

"No, you wouldn't," Duckie told her. "Since he started college, Jan's so stuck-up. Really, he's always telling me that I don't care about the right things. Humpf," she said in disgust. "If that's not the pot calling the kitten black, I don't know what is!"

This time, Duckie's verbal mix-up was funnier.

Darby didn't realize she'd giggled out loud until the Viking whirled around.

"What's so funny?" Duckie demanded.

Darby swallowed with difficulty. Angry, her cousin looked even bigger — monstrous, even. Darby knew she couldn't stand up to her. Though Darby almost never played dumb, this time it meant survival.

"Nothing! Oh, my gosh! Did I walk right past A Building?" Darby squeaked. "I'm trying to find my history class and I don't know if I'm going the right way." Darby pretended to study her schedule.

"You don't have history now," Duckie said before turning to Selena. "How do you like this? I know her schedule better than she does!"

The other girls tittered with laughter.

"You have P.E., remember?" Selena reminded her.

"Oh, yeah," Darby crowed as if the realization had just struck her.

Another of Duckie's friends, a girl with professionally streaked hair, leaned back with her arms crossed, raised one eyebrow, and stared toward Darby's feet. "Nice boots."

Darby ignored the sarcasm as Duckie's group crowded into the gym ahead of her.

Megan was dressed and just tying her shoes when she looked up at Darby.

"Hi!" Darby said.

"Hi." Megan sounded startled by Darby's enthusiasm. "You look like you're about to throw yourself into my arms."

"I'm glad to see a friendly face," Darby admitted as she opened her locker and changed clothes.

Megan didn't bother asking what had brought on that remark, because Duckie leaned around the bank of lockers and jerked her thumb toward Darby to say, "Tell your friend we don't wear cowboy boots to school."

Megan ignored the big girl and sat down on a nearby bench. Letting her hands dangle between her knees, Megan faced Darby and said, "Remember that thing Jonah said last night?"

"About a flea making an elephant squirm?" Darby asked.

"Something like that," Megan said with a laugh.

"Thanks for reminding me," Darby said, but before she could ask Megan for suggestions, she was off with her soccer friends, leaving Darby behind.

Since staying invisible didn't seem to be working for her, Darby cast around in her brain for another strategy to make herself a less amusing victim.

*I'll kill you with kindness*, Darby thought the minute she saw Duckie heading her way.

"I love your earrings! What are they?" Darby asked, even though she recognized them as black pearls.

"They're none of your business," Duckie said, reaching up to touch one of her earrings.

"Duxelles, why don't you put those in your locker? You don't want to lose one while you're playing volleyball."

Both girls turned to see Miss Day striding toward them, on her way outside.

"Thanks, Coach Day," Duckie said sweetly, "but I'll be careful."

"Do it now, please," Miss Day told her.

"Yes, Coach Day," Duckie said, but as soon as the teacher had passed, Duckie shot Darby a glare.

Darby pretended interest in her stubby fingernails and kept walking as the big girl started back to the locker room.

Outside, Darby rushed to take her place on the blacktop, but she needn't have hurried. It was clear that Coach Roffmore wouldn't take roll until his favorite student showed up.

Darby was dreading Duckie's return when she noticed Coach Roffmore looking right at her.

It was such a direct and positive look that Darby glanced over her shoulder in surprise. But the coach was talking to her.

"Carter. Your transfer papers say you're a swimmer."

All at once, Darby realized he was sizing her up as an addition to his team.

"I used to be," Darby said.

There was no point in joining a team when she might not be at this school long enough to compete. Besides, Megan had told her Duckie was on the swim team. The prospect of swimming with Duckie and her friends was about as appealing as joining a school of sharks.

Darby kept her eyes forward, pretending not to notice Duckie jostling into line.

When Selena giggled behind her, Darby turned around to see what was so funny.

"All eyes on me," the coach snapped, but Darby couldn't help glancing down the line to see if Megan had noticed anything.

Duckie was quick, but out of the corner of her eye, Darby saw her arm drop back to her side. Duckie faced forward with military straightness, but her lips smirked.

"Knock it off," Darby whispered.

"I bet I could," Duckie said, squinting at Darby's head.

Darby couldn't let the big girl get away with bullying her.

"All eyes on me!" Coach Roffmore shouted when Darby kept staring at the big girl.

Darby took a deep breath, then appealed to the coach. "Did you see what she did?"

"I'm gonna see you running laps if you don't stop disrupting my class, Carter."

"Yeah, Cowgirl Carter," Selena sneered from behind her.

Darby's cheeks burned at the unfairness, and she knew Selena wasn't the only one staring at her.

Megan leaned forward in line to catch Darby's eye, but her frown didn't offer any advice.

"I didn't figure you for a troublemaker," the coach added.

It was his faint disappointment that got to her.

"I'm sorry," Darby apologized, but as the coach continued calling roll, Darby's eyes slid sideways.

Watching her cousin, Darby tried to come up with another way this flea could make the Viking tyrannosaurus squirm.

She hadn't come up with a single idea when Duckie yanked Darby's ponytail and it came loose from its holder.

The surprise on the big girl's face probably meant she hadn't planned to jerk the ponytail that hard, but

Darby didn't care what her cousin had *meant* to do.

"Keep your hands to yourself, Duckie!" Darby roared.

She heard a shocked whoop of approval that might have been Megan. A female voice muttered, "Right on," and a short-lived spate of clapping ended when the coach tweeted his whistle.

"That's it." Coach Roffmore pointed at the track. "Give me a mile."

"Two laps," Coach Day corrected, saying something behind her clipboard to Coach Roffmore.

"Gimme two," he agreed.

And Darby did.

Chapter 11

During lunch, Darby stood by in uncomfortable silence as Megan and her friends surrounded Ann and praised the stand Darby had taken against her cousin.

"She was so cool walking over to the track." Megan imitated Darby with long, ambling steps. "She just moseyed over there, putting her ponytail back up, taking her time . . ."

*Trying not to cry*, Darby added mentally.

She'd been afraid to run a half-mile while crying. What if she started wheezing and passed out or something?

Now Darby just listened and spooned yogurt into her mouth. If she were a different person, she'd be pleased with all this admiration.

As it was, she felt worried.

By the time Darby had run two sweaty laps and made her way to the sandpits where the girls were playing volleyball, all but Duckie's closest friends were giggling about Darby's stubbornness.

Someone had even created a hand gesture — bringing the tips of all four fingers down to touch the pad of the thumb. If you opened and closed it quickly, your hand looked like a quacking duck.

It was clearly meant to be a silent mockery of Duxelles's new nickname.

"So Duckie's plan to humiliate you kinda backfired," Ann said, giving Darby a congratulatory pat on the back.

"Kinda, but I'm pretty sure she won't take it as a learning experience."

"Probably not," Ann agreed, and there was troubled comprehension in her eyes.

Neither of them uttered the word *payback*, but Darby was pretty sure they were both thinking it; Duckie wouldn't let this offense go.

"She didn't even think of backing down from Duckie or Roffmore," said Tabby, one of the soccer girls who'd been Ann's teammate, too.

"How could Coach Roffmore not see what she did?" Ann asked.

"He saw," Megan assured her. "He just didn't care."

Darby wished she didn't have to face the coach and Duckie in algebra.

"The only way you'd get Roffmore to care . . ." Megan's voice trailed off for a second. Tilting her head to one side, Megan licked a dab of milk shake off her lip. ". . . is if you proved you were a better swimmer than Duckie."

"How good are you?" Ann asked Darby.

Megan answered for her, "She's *good*."

Megan had never seen her swim, but she said it in a way that reminded Darby that Megan knew she'd swum in the ocean with Hoku.

"Not that good," Darby said, but her voice was drowned out by the bell ringing, ending lunchtime.

After school, Darby stalled.

While she waited for Aunty Cathy to come collect her and Megan, she walked between the soccer field, where Megan's team played, and the wooden picnic table outside the chain-link fence surrounding the school swimming pool.

As the girls' swim team warmed up, Darby breathed in the scent of chlorine.

It made her homesick. And impatient.

When she saw Duckie roll the muscles in her tanned shoulders, Darby thought of her own arms slicing through the water.

Duckie dove into the pool, and though the girl was good—you didn't get to be a regional champion in Hawaii if you were only *okay*—inside her cowgirl boots, Darby pointed her toes and imagined her own powerful kick.

She wanted to join the swim team for all the wrong reasons.

Darby remembered Ann pointing out the single pay telephone on the campus, right in front of the school, where Aunty Cathy dropped them off in the morning.

On impulse, Darby found it and called her mother's cell phone. Her mother was so glad to hear from her, she didn't even mention that she'd called collect.

"Baby! How did you know I was lonesome for your voice? What's up?"

Darby told her mother about watching swim practice while she waited out Megan's soccer practice. Her mother heard the longing in her voice before Darby got very far.

"Would you like to join? For just a little while?"

"No . . ."

"Just today, in one of the shops, I saw a gorgeous red tank suit like the ones you and Heather always talked about." Her mother's wheedling tone made Darby hope that her mother wanted her—or both of them!—to remain on the island.

"Do you think we might stay here?" Darby asked.

"Stay . . . ?"

"In Hawaii," Darby said.

"Oh, no, no, no!" Her mother laughed. "I just want you to make the most of it while you are."

Well, she hadn't *really* thought that was a possibility, anyway. Still, what if her mother had forgotten the beauty of 'Iolani Ranch and outgrown her feud with Jonah?

"But if I *do* earn the reward for finding Stormbird, you know, that lost colt? And I bought you a ticket to here, you'd come visit, right?"

"I'll think about it, honey."

The scratchy connection stretched between them, and Darby knew from experience that she should quit while she was ahead.

"Bye, Mom. I love you," she said finally.

"I love you, too!"

Once she'd hung up, Darby's mind spun.

*No way. Why join the swim team?*

She smiled because her mother had remembered the bright red tank suits she and Heather had chatted about. They'd considered them signs that they were good swimmers so they wouldn't be afraid to stand out.

But her mother had been right, Darby thought. She should make the most of her time in Hawaii. That meant spending time with Hoku.

Darby was still standing by the pay phone when a big white car — maybe an Escalade — pulled over. It sounded as if an entire Hawaiian band was playing inside.

Darby watched as a tinted window lowered auto-matically. The ukuleles and warbling singers inside the car stopped, and Darby realized she almost rec-ognized the driver.

"Aloha!" the woman called, looking even more familiar as she removed her dark glasses. "Are you Ellen Kealoha's girl?"

The woman referring to her mother by her unmarried name, with her stylishly shingled black hair, Hawaiian features, and orange lipstick, was Babe Borden.

"Yes, but how did you know?" Darby asked.

"For once in his life, my brother was right. Jonah said you look just like your mother."

*Impossible*, Darby thought. Her mother was a movie star.

Still, the words sent a thrill through her.

"Trust me, dear, you do," Babe told her. "And then, there are your boots."

Darby looked down at her honey-brown boots and smiled.

"If you were thinking about walking home, you couldn't have reached it before dark. Hop in and I'll give you a lift."

"Oh, no, I wasn't. I was just, uh . . ." Darby was gesturing toward the phone when she heard the lock on the door next to her pop.

Despite Jonah's railing against her, Darby thought she might like Babe. She didn't admire her because she looked more stylish than anyone else Darby had seen on the island; she liked her because Aunt Babe had noticed her cowgirl boots.

Her short, shiny hair didn't show a thread of Jonah's gray, and she was dressed all in white. Her car was white with muted gold trim.

If she owned Sugar Sands Cove Resort, all the white made sense. It was obviously her trademark, just as Megan had said, and Darby didn't blame Babe for being a good businesswoman.

Best of all, with Aunt Babe's help, Darby figured she could be home before Megan, in time to saddle Navigator and Tango. All she had to do was get in.

"Just let me go tell Megan what's up," Darby told her great-aunt, and the minute Babe nodded, Darby sprinted back to the soccer field.

At once, she spotted Megan on the sideline.

Perfect, Darby thought, even though Megan was poised with the black-and-white ball above her head, about to throw it in.

"I've got a ride home," Darby yelled.

"What?" Megan sounded bewildered, as if Darby had broken her concentration.

"Aunt Babe is giving me a ride home."

"Okay," Megan said. Then she threw and bolted back into the action of the practice game.

"Thanks," Darby said breathlessly when she'd returned.

As she climbed inside, the scents of white linen

and citrus surrounded her. It smelled like luxury.

Darby settled into the lush leather seat.

If Jonah got mad at her for allowing Babe to drive her home, well, it probably wouldn't last long. Soon, Darby would be bringing home a colt worth a substantial reward from Babe.

"I was on my way to pick up Duxelles," Babe began, before she pulled away from the curb.

"Oh, well, go ahead, I can—"

"I'm forty minutes early," Babe told her. "I was going to sit and read while I waited, but this is much better. I have something to show you."

Darby caught her breath as Babe made a U-turn in the middle of the street.

"Don't worry, I'm an expert driver," Babe said as they sped in the opposite direction from 'Iolani Ranch. "Now, I've heard you love horses."

"I do."

"Then I must introduce you to my mare Flight."

Darby recognized the horse's name immediately. She was Stormbird's mother.

"I heard what happened to her colt," Darby said.

"I invited Jonah over to see if he could help, but your grandfather did nothing to soothe her," Babe said.

Darby wasn't sure if she heard anger or concern in Babe's voice, but if her great-aunt expected more from her than Jonah, she'd be disappointed.

"I'm not a horse charmer," Darby apologized.

"Of course you're not. Trust me, dear, there is no such family gift."

Was that the second or third time her great-aunt had said "trust me, dear"? Every time she said that, it had the opposite effect.

Babe glanced over at Darby. "I don't expect you to do anything. I just want to show off."

"Oh."

"Your grandfather's probably told you that I'm a voracious social climber who cares only for money, because I've never outgrown having to collect road-kill."

Babe didn't sound offended. In fact, her tone was so cheery, Darby had to replay the words to make sure she understood.

*Voracious social climber*. Did that mean Aunt Babe was starving to improve her status? *Caring only for money*. That was simple enough. But . . . *roadkill*?

"He never told me anything like that," Darby said.

Babe's deep chuckling laugh reminded Darby of Tutu. Though Aunt Babe was Tutu's daughter, Darby had a hard time reconciling this totally modern woman with a great-grandmother who lived with an owl in the middle of the rain forest.

"He hasn't?" Babe sounded incredulous. "Are you sure?"

"Well, he mentioned the money part," Darby admitted. "But that's all."

As they raced down the highway, Darby remembered Kimo driving her from the airport to the ranch.

Black lava fields flanked the road, and Darby didn't think they were far from the resort Kimo had pointed out, so Darby decided she had to ask. "What did you mean, exactly, about roadkill?"

Babe tossed her head, as if she had long hair.

"I assume Jonah hasn't gotten rid of our father's fox cages yet?" Babe asked.

Surprised at the direction the conversation with Babe had taken, Darby said, "They're still there."

"They used to house foxes, obviously, and the first week I had my driver's license, our father saw an opportunity to put me to work doing something new."

Babe's tone was grim, until she added, "And highly profitable."

Babe shook her head as she went on, "Foxes are totally carnivorous, as you undoubtedly know. So feeding them is pretty pricey."

Darby's brain balked. Aunt Babe couldn't mean that her father had sent her out to gather creatures that had been hit by cars?

Babe glanced toward Darby with eyebrows raised so high, they arched above the frames of her dark glasses.

"Trust me, dear, nothing improves a girl's social standing or attracts more boyfriends than cruising around in an old farm truck, picking up dead animals."

Babe's practiced sarcasm didn't keep an involuntary shudder from shaking her shoulders.

Aunt Babe was kind of stuck-up and phony, but Darby felt a little sorry for the girl she'd been. Still, the only thing that she could think of to say was, "Yuck."

"Yuck, indeed," Babe Borden said. Her manicured nails glittered as her hands swept over the steering wheel, bringing them into a gated resort.

The sparkling hotel might have been molded out of sugar. It rose from a pristine white beach to stand silhouetted against the bright blue waters beyond.

It was a different kind of beautiful than 'Iolani Ranch, Darby thought, but still pretty amazing.

"Welcome to Sugar Sands Cove Resort," Babe said. "Let me introduce you to Flight."

Chapter 12

When the Escalade pulled up in front of Sugar Sands Cove Resort's stable and paddock, Darby noticed Babe's fence was identical to the one surrounding 'Iolani Ranch.

That made her smile, as she thought Aunt Babe and Jonah might not be so different after all.

Darby's smile turned into awe when she saw the cremellos.

Six glossy, well-tended white horses—no, seven—waited in the paddock, looking eager for a ride.

Were these the horses Babe planned to give Jonah as the start of a dude string? Was she generous enough to allow tourists to ride her prized horses for a fee?

Most of the horses ranged from stark white to cream, but one had a tawny coat. Darby might have guessed his coat was just washed with sunlight, if his white blaze hadn't set it off.

All seven cremellos had flaxen manes and tails and slim, leggy conformation.

The most beautiful horse of the bunch stood apart from the others, close to the fence.

"This is Flight," Babe told Darby.

Until now, Darby had felt anxious about heading in the opposite direction from 'Iolani Ranch. She'd been polite to her great-aunt, of course, and she was intrigued by the resort, but impatience had gnawed at her, urging her to get back to the ranch, saddle up Navigator, and find Stormbird.

All that vanished when Darby saw the grieving mare.

Flight's white coat was spotless. Her pale gold mane and tail had been brushed free of tangles. But she didn't prance with pride. Her silken mane and forelock drifted across her face like a mourning veil as she paced the fence, ignoring the extra food set out for her.

Every few strides, she paused to give long nickers.

*How long has she been doing this?* Darby wondered, noticing the huskiness of the mare's cries.

Flight stopped just feet away from Darby. Raising her head and pricking her ears, the mare stared into the distance, listening for an answer from her lost foal.

Babe gravitated to the mare, as if she had no choice, and the horse came to her, shoving urgently against the fence.

Babe made a helpless gesture.

"I don't know what she expects. I'm doing all I can. Everyone I know is out looking for Stormbird. I'd be out there myself if I weren't here working for your feed, wouldn't I, baby?"

Babe reached through the fence to pet the horse, then cleared her throat.

"You're just a drab-coated bag of bones, aren't you, girl?"

Babe's way of pairing harsh words with gentle actions reminded Darby of Jonah, too.

Darby remembered how he'd sworn at Hoku even as he dove into sharp strands of barbed wire to cut her free.

"Did the other horses edge her out of the herd, or is she a loner?" Darby asked.

"A little of both," Babe told her. "She was gone for a while, being trained on Maui, and since her return, Flight's been so sad, I think the herd bonds are sort of strained."

*Being trained?* Flight's jutting ribs and the hollows above her eyes made her look too old for special training.

"She's only five," Babe said, following the direction

of Darby's gaze. "I have to find her colt or she's not going to make it."

Darby had been eager to track down Stormbird before, but now she was desperate, and her desperation had nothing to do with money.

It was hard not to tell Babe that she'd seen the colt, but Darby decided she'd wait until there was no chance of disappointing her great-aunt. That would be like losing him twice.

"I'd better go," Darby said, "but you can just drop me off at school. I mean, it was so nice of you to show me your horses, and the resort," Darby said as they got back into the Escalade. When she spotted the car clock, Darby added, "It is getting late and I'm sure you don't want to keep D—"

Darby swallowed hard. She'd come so close to saying Duckie that she became tongue-tied and was unable to pronounce her cousin's real name.

"She'll be fine," Babe said.

They'd passed the turnoff to Lehua High School and gone a few miles farther when Babe raised her dark glasses, looked at Darby, and asked, "Did you hear about my plan for a riding stable at 'Iolani?"

"Yes," Darby answered, and though she didn't mean to set her jaw and go silent, that's just what she did.

"Not you, too." Babe sounded surprised. "You absolutely echoed Jonah's tone of voice. Next you'll be saying it's a betrayal of our native heritage."

Babe didn't sound disappointed, just resigned to the fact that it would take them both a while to come around to her way of thinking.

"Your mother would see the beauty of my plan," Babe said.

Darby didn't tell her that the idea had already won over Aunty Cathy and Megan.

"In fact," Babe said, shaking her index finger toward the windshield, "perhaps Ellen Kealoha Carter, my famous niece, should stay at Sugar Sands Cove with some of her celebrity friends."

Babe nodded and her lips curved in amusement, as if her imagination was spinning her idea into a star-studded fantasy.

Darby decided it would be mean to tell Aunt Babe that Mom's friends weren't celebrities, but struggling actors like she was. In fact, one of her best friends chuckled that his biggest claim to fame was when a fan magazine had dubbed him "dog walker to the stars."

Aunt Babe cleared her throat before saying, "Jonah should consider the future."

There was something morbid in Babe's tone.

"I think he does," Darby told her great-aunt. "Maybe too much. He's always—" Darby closed her mouth. It felt like a betrayal, revealing how Jonah fretted over who'd run the ranch after he was gone.

"He's always what?" Babe turned down the dirt road to the ranch.

"Considering the future," Darby repeated her great-aunt's words.

Darby was surprised when Babe braked hard at the cattle guard in front of the ranch gate and asked, "Is this close enough?"

"Sure," Darby said.

It took her a minute to grab her backpack and open the door. She was barely clear of the vehicle before Babe slammed the gear shift into reverse and left.

An hour later, Cade and Megan were following Darby's directions back to the spot where she'd seen the lost colt. This time they wore maile leis for luck.

"I might like them even more than the flower ones," Darby had said when Cade hung the strand of leaves in a horseshoe around her neck.

Leathery pointed leaves ran in pairs along a vine, which hung down to her elbows. Its fragrance struck Darby as a combination of vanilla and pine.

"You *made* these?" Darby asked.

"They're traditional for paniolos, just twisted together," Cade said. He fiddled absently with the keeper on his rope as if Darby were making too much of the simple lei. "But I was thinking the colt might be more comfortable with us if we smell, uh, not just human, but natural."

"Good idea," Megan told him.

"Thanks, Cade," Darby said, but she wished Cade

hadn't brought his rifle.

*Your reaction is totally irrational,* Darby told herself.

A dangerous wild boar had proven that just last week. A weapon could be vital in rough country, and parts of Wild Horse Island still counted as wilderness. If Cade hadn't put the rabid animal down, it might have hurt Hoku, Navigator, or Tango.

As they rode through the forest, heading for Night Digger Point Beach, something fell out of the trees and struck the ground off to their right.

Cade twisted in his saddle to face the sound.

"Relax, Lone Ranger," Megan joked, "it was just a candlenut falling."

Despite Megan's crack about Cade acting like a gunslinger, he rode on with one hand holding his reins and the other on his rifle scabbard.

A gust of salty wind blew at them from Night Digger Point Beach, and Darby knew they were getting close.

Megan turned toward Darby and mused, "I wonder if you're the only one who's seen him."

"Me too," Darby admitted. "When I met Aunt Babe, she didn't say anyone else had reported seeing him."

"You didn't tell her *you* had," Cade said.

"No." Darby wondered why Cade sounded as sure as if he'd been there.

"Probably not, then," Megan said, but she didn't catch Cade's superior look.

*What's that about?* Darby asked herself, but the others rode quickly, trying to beat the night, and she had all she could do to match their pace.

As they rode onto Night Digger Point Beach, Darby was struck again by its lack of greenness.

If she'd been any place besides Wild Horse Island, that might not have seemed remarkable, but in Hawaii it was rare to see a place where you'd only need three colors to paint a landscape: blue, white, and black.

Blue water, black sand, and white-capped waves, that is.

"It's a good thing we rode out tonight," Megan told them. "My mom says a storm's on its way."

Blue sky shadowed with black clouds made a background for white birds winging inland.

"He needs to take shelter, " Darby said, and suddenly the three colors of the place rang like an alarm. "If there's nothing green here, what he's been eating?"

"He'll be hungry," Cade said.

All at once Darby wondered if she'd been naive about the colt's chance for survival without his mother to give him milk.

When were foals weaned from milk to grass? In the back of her mind, she thought Sam Forster had said that her filly, Tempest, hadn't been weaned until she was six months old!

"If he's really only three or four months old, has

he been weaned?" Darby asked gingerly.

"He has now," Cade said.

"Don't be mean," Megan said to Cade. Then, standing in her stirrups as she looked out to sea, Megan said, "Hey, Darby, I think I saw a mermaid."

Darby brushed aside Megan's silly attempt to distract her. "There's not much to eat around here, is there? You don't think he starved, do you?"

"Didn't you say he was playful?" Cade asked.

"Yes, but that was two days ago."

"Obviously he'd been eating *something* if he was having a good time with Navigator," Megan said.

Wild horses *were* pretty resourceful, Darby thought. But this colt wasn't wild; just alone.

 Chapter 13

"I'm sure Stormbird's okay," Megan said. "It's a small island and everyone talks. If someone else had spotted him—dead or alive—my mom would have heard about it at the post office or grocery store."

Darby glanced at Cade again, and this time so did Megan.

"Why are you looking like that? Don't you think we would have heard?" Megan demanded.

"Of course not," Cade said. "There's money involved."

"Oh, yeah," Darby said. For her, this was about saving two horses. Of course she'd take the money, but she'd be searching for Stormbird even if there was no reward.

But Cade was right. They couldn't count on everyone feeling that way.

The beach was empty, stripped bare by low tide. They would have seen something as big as a horse.

Darby's mood sank as they spread out, looking for hoofprints.

With the sun submerged, the beach turned evening blue. The retreating waves had left the sand shrouded in white foam. Overhead, a black bird hovered.

*It's huge,* Darby thought, looking up so high that her ponytail touched the back of her belt.

And the bird was watching something.

Darby scanned the beach, but didn't see anything. She figured the bird must be interested in something that meant nothing to her—maybe a bubble signaling a tasty sand creature.

And then there were two black birds. No, three.

They looked like big black *X*s, Darby thought, with the top bars slightly bent and the bottom bars shrunken.

As the threesome wheeled closer, Darby saw that the top of the *X* was formed by huge wings. She'd bet they were six or seven feet across. And the bottom of the *X* was a fanned tail with longer feathers at each side.

"What kind of birds are those?" Darby shouted down the beach to Megan.

"I can't remember," Megan yelled back, then rode Tango toward Navigator as she continued, "We usually see them in summer. After the baby turtles hatch,

while they're scurrying toward the water, they"—
Megan pointed upward—"eat them, or snatch them
up to carry them back to their nests."

The flock lifted at the human voices, but not for
long. The next time they lowered, the birds let out a
raucous chorus of discovery.

What had they found? Darby wondered. Then,
over the birds' excited shrieking, she heard something else.

A slap and a splash almost made her think she'd
heard a seal, but Navigator told her otherwise.

His deep-chested neigh drew nickers from Tango
and Joker.

On the other side of the volcanic rock with the
tide pool on top, there was a scoop, like maybe
another ancient bubble had popped there. Nestled
into its shelter was Stormbird.

"I found him!" Darby hissed at Megan, even
though the older girl was too far away to hear.

Darby pointed, and then she, Cade, and Megan
jostled for the best views of the colt.

When Cade didn't reach for his rope, Darby
asked, "Now what?" Even those two words, spoken
in a normal voice, startled the colt.

Stormbird bolted to his feet.

*We can't lose him now,* Darby thought.

The colt wobbled on long legs, then leaned
against the rock as if he yearned to run, but couldn't.

Cade and Megan looked at each other and exchanged some silent sign that Darby didn't understand.

Megan dismounted. Her boots hit the wet beach with a splat. When Darby started to get off Navigator, Megan shook her head, then threw her reins to Cade.

Megan hummed and sang as she approached the colt. Darby couldn't hear the lyrics at first, but all four horses listened.

Eventually Darby picked up enough words to understand that Megan sang of a woman wading in a lagoon and scooping up tiny fish; and of a goddess wading across the sky scooping up silver stars.

Whatever it meant, the colt was soothed. Megan repeated her lullaby, as she slipped the maile lei inch by inch off her own neck, and eased it over Stormbird's.

At last, Megan edged back toward the other horses, and Stormbird came with her.

*He seems hypnotized*, Darby thought. *And weak.*

Was Stormbird sick? Had he run out of food? Was he missing Flight as much as she missed him?

Darby was barely able to hold back her questions, but she did, afraid another sound would make the colt jerk against the slender vine and break it.

Cade lifted his canteen off his saddle. He extended it, along with a bandanna, toward Megan.

Megan shrugged, but Darby understood.

They all knew that the colt needed water. After all, how could a barn-raised baby find his own fresh water when he was surrounded by an ocean?

Silently begging Navigator not to wander away, Darby slipped off the big horse, snagged the canteen and bandanna from Megan, and started toward the colt.

Stormbird's head jerked up.

Even in twilight, his eyes shone turquoise. They stared at her with alarm and then looked past her.

Darby heard Navigator's hooves. The gelding wasn't deserting her, he was following, and that should make her task much easier.

*Yes!* she thought. Just as before, the colt was enchanted with Navigator.

Darby held her hands low, unscrewed the top of the canteen, and poured a tiny pool of water in her hand.

Sidetracked by the wonderful smell, the colt butted at her hands and spilled the water.

If he wanted it, why didn't he lick it from her hands? Darby poured more water into her palm and held it under the colt's mouth.

His impossibly soft lips rubbed over her hand. Then, he took a step back, and he shook his head in frustration when Megan's hand snaked the bandanna slowly from Darby's belt. Then Megan dipped one end into the canteen.

*Of course!* Darby thought. The colt hadn't been trained to drink from a bucket or lick from someone's hand. He'd still been nursing when he was separated from his mother.

Megan wiped the wet cloth over the colt's mouth. He licked his lips and immediately understood.

*He's a smart little guy,* Darby thought as Stormbird pulled noisily on the end of the wet bandanna.

In seconds, the colt was sucking for water. Megan couldn't get the bandanna away from him to rewet it until it tickled his throat and Stormbird coughed.

With flying fingers, Megan dipped the bandanna again. She'd hardly withdrawn it when the cremello colt lurched forward, ready for more.

"He's too big to put over my saddle," Cade said quietly, but Darby could tell he didn't want to scare the colt by roping him.

The colt looked at him from under white eye-lashes, but he was too thirsty to care about the creature atop the Appaloosa horse.

Darby nodded toward Navigator and raised her eyebrows. Cade considered the gelding.

Navigator was the biggest and calmest of the three saddle horses. If any of the horses could carry a live load, it would be him.

But Cade gave a skeptical head shake, and so did Megan.

Measuring herself against the colt, Darby realized his legs were as long as hers. Even if she, Megan, and Cade worked together and managed to get the colt across Navigator's back, Stormbird would struggle. A chance strike from one of his hooves meant someone would be hurt.

Finally, through a series of signs and whispers, they worked a soft loop of rope over Stormbird's neck, but didn't tighten it.

They'd take turns walking with the colt, guiding him with the maile lei, and only use the rope in an emergency.

At least that's what Darby got out of their pantomime, and now she reveled in her turn to walk with Stormbird.

Warm winds swirled around her, and once they left the beach, trees blew and bowed and showered them with sweet scents.

Energized by sips of water, the colt showed every sign that he'd have no trouble walking back to the ranch.

"What we need is a song or story," she told the colt. His ears cupped toward her.

Stormbird had enjoyed Megan's song. If Darby had known it, she would have sung it again. Since she didn't, she tried to think of something similar instead.

"Got it!" she told him. "A poem is almost like a song."

Taking a deep breath, Darby recited, "Wynken, Blynken, and Nod one night sailed off in a wooden shoe—sailed on a river of crystal light, into a sea of dew. . . ."

The colt tossed his muzzle skyward, but it wasn't like he was trying to get away. He almost seemed to be pointing.

Darby looked up to see a rainbow circle around the moon.

"Good boy," she said, and then she went on, "The old moon laughed and sang a song . . ." Darby had forgotten a few lines, but she figured Stormbird wouldn't mind, so she just picked up again where she could.

"The little stars were the herring-fish that lived in the beautiful sea. Now cast your nets wherever you wish—never afeard are we! . . ."

Cade looked back at her from his position on Joker's back.

Moonlight and shadows didn't give her a very good view of his face, so she couldn't tell what he thought of her reciting.

But his good opinion wasn't the one she was after.

Darby was singing for Stormbird, keeping his spirits up until he was back with his mother, and he liked her serenade so well, he bumped shoulders with her as if she were another horse.

"Just wait until I introduce you to Hoku," Darby told the colt. "It's the logical place for us to put you.

We can't just turn you loose with the other foals and their moms, can we?"

The pale colt stopped and planted his front hooves wide apart.

They'd reached the trail to the old plantation. Wind tossed the trees alongside the path, and Stormbird's nostrils opened to draw in the abundance of night scents.

Megan drew Tango to a halt, and Navigator sidled up against the rose roan mare.

"Keep chanting or whatever you were doing," Megan said quietly.

Pretending to be insulted, Darby whispered, "For your information, I was reciting poetry to Storm-bird."

Cade gave an amused snort and Megan replied, "Whatever. Just keep doing it so we can get going again."

So Darby did, skipping ahead to the next part of the poem that she remembered.

"'Twas all so pretty a sail, it seemed, as if it could not be; and some folks thought 'twas a dream they'd dreamed, of sailing that beautiful sea. . . .'"

A dream? Darby knew this was better than any dream she'd ever have.

How many people had ever strolled through a tropical paradise on a Tuesday night, with a prancing cremello and two good friends?

She tried to make a sensible estimate. Fewer than

five, she thought. At most.

Even then, she was pretty sure that no other girl in the entire history of the world had ever been so happy being exactly where she was right now.

Darby sighed and walked on toward 'Iolani Ranch.

 Chapter 14

It was dark when they got back to the ranch, but Kit and Kimo were waiting for them under the light mounted on the tack shed.

The colt was plodding along with his head down, too tired to notice his strange surroundings.

"Heard you comin'," Kit said. "Good job."

"Do you think he's too tired to travel?" Darby asked when Kimo knelt beside the weary colt.

"I think that would be pushing him," Kimo said, but by the time Darby finished describing the shape Flight was in, he and Kit looked at each other as if hoping for a solution.

"Rest him now and we'll get him over to Sugar Sands first thing in the morning," Cade suggested.

"How's that?" Kit asked.

"No trailer hitch on the Ram," Kimo said, referring to his truck.

"I'll kayak, if I have to," Cade said. "Don't want any more crazies stomping around looking for him, or stallions like Luna coming up to teach him who's boss."

"Kayak's no good with that storm coming in."

"He's already gone swimmin' once," Cade said. "Doesn't seem any worse off."

Darby and Megan tried to make sense of the choppy conversation.

Were they really considering moving the colt in a little boat?

Darby *had* seen a battered yellow kayak somewhere around the place, but she wouldn't want to share such close quarters with Stormbird.

It was quiet for a few minutes until Kit said, "Cade, you're not being sensible."

"I know it," Cade said. Then the cowboys laughed.

"Let's weld a hitch on the Ram," Kimo said. "Been meaning to do that, anyway."

"That suits me okay," Cade said.

"Do you feel invisible?" Megan asked, jerking her thumb toward the cowboys.

Darby nodded, but then she volunteered, "We'll take care of the horses," and that got their attention.

❈ ❈ ❈

Hoku's neigh woke Darby at five o'clock the next morning. She blinked at the sound of an engine starting. The instant her brain made sense of the sounds, she got out of bed and started putting on clothes as fast as she could.

It had been late when Darby had stopped watching from her bedroom window. The silver-gold sparks from the cowboys' welding had looked like fireworks, and she had no idea what time they'd gone to bed.

She guessed that Kimo had bunked with Cade and Kit in the foreman's house because they'd need his truck in the morning to get Stormbird delivered back to his mother before it was time to take the girls to school.

Darby heard tires crunch on gravel. If she didn't run, Kit would drive off without her. It didn't matter how early it was. She didn't want to miss Stormbird's reunion with his mother.

She made it.

They would have sneaked into the drowsy resort unnoticed, except for Flight.

The cream-colored mare scented her son as soon as the truck pulled up beside her corral.

Instantly, she greeted him with ear-splitting neighs.

When Stormbird responded, squealing, Kit touched the windshield.

"Wonder if he can shatter glass?" Kit asked.

The colt's whinnies echoed inside the livestock trailer until the cremellos outside neighed and ran mad laps around their paddock.

*Poor Duckie,* Darby thought, smiling at the image of her cousin wrapping a pillow around her ears to block out the noisy dawn.

Babe Borden was already up. Like the ranch girl she'd been long ago, Babe nimbly loosed Stormbird to his mother, but didn't allow the other cremellos to escape their pen.

"No media until all three of you are here," Babe said, patting Darby on the back.

Darby was watching Flight keep the other horses from a too-close inspection of the newcomer when Babe's words sunk in.

"Media?" Darby asked.

"Ah, I see you didn't read the fine print on our website." Babe said it with a smile, but she wasn't joking. "Part of the reward is contingent on doing just the smallest bit of public relations for Sugar Sands. Nothing tawdry," Babe promised.

"Oh, good," Darby said, but she wasn't sure she knew what *tawdry* even meant. Something like *tacky*, maybe.

"I'll notify everyone to call off the search and inform the media of our special award ceremony."

Darby didn't ask *when* the ceremony would take place, because suddenly, as she watched Flight and

Stormbird, Babe swallowed hard. The mare and foal curved around each other, necks all but twining together.

"Good thing no one's up yet," Babe said. She wiped the back of one hand across her eyes and glanced toward the main hotel building, hoping no one would see her being sentimental about the horses she clearly loved.

Duxelles couldn't have looked any different than Babe later that day at school.

The big girl's eyes glittered with jealousy. Instead of making a milk-gulping spectacle of herself during Nutrition Break, she and her friends made their way over to Darby and Ann.

"I've got your back," Ann said, not entirely joking.

"Good," Darby said. She stood tall, trying to look pleasantly surprised at Duckie's approach.

When she got close enough, Duxelles extended her hand.

Darby watched with dread, but when her hand opened, Duxelles only held a piece of folded green paper.

Darby took it, opened it, and read an official request for her to join the swim team. Then, she met Duckie's eyes.

"Thanks, but I can't. I need more time to work with my horse," she said honestly. "Plus, I don't think

I'll be here long enough to do the team any good."

"That's from *Coach*. He doesn't send those to everyone."

"I'll explain to him in P.E.," Darby said.

When a flicker of relief crossed Duckie's face, Darby waited for the big girl to go away. She didn't.

Darby tried shoving the paper into her jeans pocket, carelessly crumbling it so that Duckie would know she meant what she'd said.

"So, I guess you really are my cousin. My grandmother told me the whole sorry story last night."

When Selena laughed, Duckie made a gesture that invited her friends to compare the two of them and see if they wouldn't be surprised, too.

Duxelles was tall, strong, and blond, while Darby was slim, delicate, and dark.

"I've been kind of hard on you," Duckie admitted then. "We just got up on the wrong foot, and I want to apologize."

Up on the wrong . . . ?

Darby managed not to dwell on the mishmash of expressions.

"That's okay," she said, but when Duckie moved toward her, Darby took an instinctive step back, spilling some of her orange juice out of its carton and onto her white pullover sweater.

She shouldn't have worn it anyway. It was too hot. Or was she just overheated with paranoia?

Ann must have noticed Darby's distress, because

she moved a little closer and helped her struggle out of her sweater.

Duckie noticed, too, because she prolonged the awkward conversation.

"I hope you know how amazing it is," Duckie said. "You just walked right in here, the new kid, and Babe and Coach really like you."

"I hardly know either of them," Darby said. She felt needless envy quaking off the other girl. How could she stop it?

"That's the thing. Neither of them are pushovers," Duckie went on. "But they seem to like you."

Darby looked down in embarrassment, and once she'd thought of something to say, she looked up to see that Duckie and her group were already drifting away.

She let out a sigh that sounded like a steam engine or something.

"Was that as awful as I thought it was?" Darby asked Ann.

"Not if she was sincere," Ann said, squinting and fluffing her fingers through her halo of red hair. "And I suppose that's possible."

"I guess," Darby said, tying her sweater around her waist. "But why? I mean, assuming the coach thinks I'm good enough to join the team, and, well—"

"Stop being modest and spit it out," Ann urged.

Darby laughed, pretty sure she and Ann were

destined to be friends for a long time.

"Why did he have Duckie deliver the note?"

"Ask me something hard," Ann said as they walked toward their next class.

"No, really. Why?"

"Right now, she doesn't have any real competition at Lehua, or in the entire region. Coach Roffmore's thinking about using you as her rabbit."

"Rabbit?" Darby squeaked.

"You know, like in dog races, there's a rabbit that all the dogs are after, and the dog that runs fastest wins."

Even though she was pretty sure that races used mechanical rabbits, not those born with flesh and fur, Darby asked, "What happens to the rabbit?"

Ann gave Darby a gentle push between the shoulder blades to get her started down the hall, and said, "Never mind. . . ."

Darby convinced herself Duckie's apology had been genuine, and she made a point of letting Duckie overhear her conversation with Coach Roffmore and Coach Day. They urged her to swim for Lehua High School, while Darby made excuses for not doing it.

When the shower bell rang, ending the last volleyball game and sending the girls inside to change clothes before lunch, Darby really thought things were looking up, because she'd made it through her P.E. class without being bullied.

But it turned out she was wrong.

Darby didn't pay much attention when Duckie slammed her locker door and stormed around, yelling something like, "Anyone can post anything on the Internet!"

Darby couldn't wait to get out of the steamy gym for lunch. She was simply glad not to be Duckie's target this time.

Darby was rushing down to the showers, still wearing her sneakers, when she tripped, then heard a splat behind her.

Duckie looked like she was kneeling on the concrete floor.

"Are you okay?" Darby asked her cousin, but then, as Darby tugged up the back of her shoe, she realized what had happened. Duckie had stepped on Darby's heel, trying to give her a "flat tire," and had fallen.

*That's what you get,* she thought, but she didn't say a thing. In fact, she'd pretty much forgotten about it until she was making her way back to her locker.

Some uproar was going on over by the coach's office, but Darby was thinking of the lovely way that Hoku's neck had curved over the white colt the previous night.

Darby was smiling when Coach Day stood on her office steps and called, "Darby? Did you push Duxelles down?"

The locker room fell silent as Duckie cupped her

hand over a skinned knee.

"No. Of course I didn't."

Coach Day shrugged at Duckie. "I'm sure it was just an accident."

The hubbub started up again, and Duckie had to yell over it.

"It wasn't an accident!"

Darby was on the verge of explaining about the flat tire when a soccer friend of Megan's said, with mock sympathy, "I think Duckie's just a little upset because Darby's swimming times are better than hers. Coach posted them side-by-side online."

First the girls' voices rose in interest; then there were mocking shouts mixed with swimmers defending their school champion.

Darby edged toward her locker.

"Girls, go to lunch," Coach Day urged them. "We have a soccer game after school today, and the team needs a few million carbs."

Duckie's face flushed red, then scarlet and almost purple.

Most of the girls moved toward the cafeteria, but they shot final glances over their shoulders on the way out.

"Now, you two," Coach Day began.

"Coach, you know she didn't—" Megan began.

"Megan, go eat," Miss Day said.

"But, Coach, come on!"

"Out," Coach Day ordered her. Then she turned

to Duxelles and Darby. "Miss Borden, Miss Carter, it would be really great if you girls could work this out on your own."

*That's hopeless,* Darby thought, and a glance at Coach Day told her the young teacher wasn't much more optimistic.

"If you could, I wouldn't have to make a report to the discipline dean, and neither of you would lose your sports eligibility."

For a minute Darby thought she felt heat blasting off Duckie's body, but she probably imagined it.

Chapter 15

By the time Darby got home, she knew what *obsessed* meant. She was a walking definition of it. All she wanted was time with her horse.

When the bell rang, Megan headed for the team bus and yelled, "See you at the game!", but Darby didn't answer.

She already knew she wouldn't ride to the soccer game in Hapuna with Jonah and Aunty Cathy in Kimo's truck.

She felt muddled and downhearted, and only time with Hoku would help. Even though Hoku had ignored Darby to groom the colt with her teeth and tongue last night, Darby knew things would be better today.

Darby changed into jeans and a gray T-shirt, then ran down to rake out Hoku's corral. The horse was usually frightened of the rake, but today she'd try to show the filly that it meant her no harm.

But once she was inside the corral, Darby gave up before she'd begun. Leaning against her rake, Darby stared at her beautiful sorrel filly.

Yesterday, Hoku had ignored her in favor of Stormbird.

She wasn't going to try training her horse today for the same reason she wouldn't tighten her ponytail in the secret sign Hoku had taught her. What if Hoku still ignored her?

*Nope, I just don't have the heart for it,* Darby thought toward her horse. *If you didn't come to me today, I don't think I could take it.*

Darby had finished feeding Hoku and Francie the fainting goat, and was calling for the five Aussie dogs when she smelled a delicious aroma coming from the bunkhouse.

Bart, the youngest Australian shepherd, smelled it, too. Wiggling his nose, he jumped up and planted his paws on Darby's shoulders as if she had the food hidden somewhere.

"Get off," she told him, and he did, but he still stood there with his head tilted to one side, wagging his tail.

Just then, Kit came out onto the porch.

"Didn't go to Megan's game," he observed.

"No, I wouldn't have been very good company."

"Some days are like that," the foreman said. "Finish up with the dogs, then come in for some real Nevada chili if ya want."

"That's the best thing I've heard all day," Darby said.

When her attention wandered for those few seconds, Bart jumped up again.

"Fine," Kit said, "if Bart don't knock you down and devour you, come on in."

Darby had never been inside the bunkhouse, but she instantly felt at home.

As she washed her hands at the kitchen sink, she glanced around.

The house was designed for a bigger staff of paniolos. Bunk beds filled about half the house while the other half had a kitchen and sitting room.

Cade was clearly surprised to see her sitting at the table, but he only nodded, and then he went to the sink to wash up, too.

"Scraped those knuckles," Kit observed as Cade winced at the sting of soap on his hand.

"Yeah," Cade said, but he didn't elaborate.

Remembering that she'd only had a granola bar for breakfast, had spilled most of her Nutrition Break orange juice, and skipped lunch, Darby decided that conversation could wait.

Kit set four bowls, a cast-iron pot of cubed beef covered with a dark red sauce, and a ladle on the table. He added a basket of hot bread, just as Kimo came in with a six-pack of sodas.

He gave her a wink and handed her one.

"I thought you went to Hapuna with Aunty Cathy and Jonah," Darby said.

"Call me crazy, but I loaned 'em my truck," Kimo said.

After that, they were all quiet. Kit's chili was incredible, and though it was spicy enough to make Darby's eyes water and nose run, she'd been raised in Southern California, where Mexican food was common, and she thought it tasted delicious.

So did the others, judging by communication that was limited to the refilling of bowls and a few appreciative nods toward Kit.

Darby leaned back in her chair and was feeling almost sleepy. Her eyes were closed when she heard Cade ask Kit if he was going to the feed store first thing tomorrow morning.

"Nope," Kit said.

Darby heard him pour coffee, and opened her eyes to see that he'd placed a cup of it, rich with cream and sugar, next to her hand.

The men waited for the foreman to explain.

"We're using the big stock trailer so we can take Hoku—"

"Hoku?" Darby interrupted.

"Yep. Been talking to Jonah. Sugar Sands has a perfect beach for water-workin' your filly."

"I don't know . . ." Darby began.

"I do," Kit said. He leaned back in his chair and half-closed his eyes, holding his coffee cup in one hand. "Water training's the best for horse and rider, and if Hawaiians *and* my people do it, how can you think it won't work?"

"Hawaiians and Native Americans both work horses in water?" Darby asked.

Kit nodded. "Takes too much energy to buck in water up to your chest, so it usually doesn't last long, and if you fall off into the water, it's nothing compared to hittin' the ground."

"The way my dad tells it," Kimo said, "in the old days, all the horses were trained in the water because that's how they shipped out cattle—roped 'em up to a draft horse and swum them out to the ships."

"Amazing." Darby sighed. "But can't we try someplace else? I don't want to go over to the Sugar Sands."

"Up to you," Cade said. "'Course, Duckie'll be expecting you to hide your head and act ashamed even though you didn't do nothing."

"What?" Darby demanded. "How did you find out about that?" But the men only laughed again.

"We have our sources, yeah?" Kimo said, but it wasn't really a question.

Chapter 16

𝓗appy that the cowboys refused her help with washing dishes and clearing up, Darby strolled across the ranch yard toward Sun House.

Jonah, Aunty Cathy, and Megan must have stopped at a restaurant for dinner, she thought, but she'd match Kit's chili against anything they were having in town.

Darby smiled into the darkening ranch yard as Francie greeted her with a shivering *naa* sound. Otherwise, the night was still.

It was so quiet, she heard the whisper of wings, and looked up to see pueo, the owl, coasting toward his favorite tree next to Hoku's corral.

Even though Sun House was empty except for her, Darby didn't stay up to watch television or investigate Jonah's library.

She'd go to bed early so that she'd be strong for tomorrow. It was one thing to daydream about riding Hoku and another to attempt it.

Darby left a note propped up on the kitchen table for Megan—then added Jonah and Aunty Cathy—asking if anyone would like to go with her and Kit to Sugar Sands Cove Resort in the morning to introduce Hoku to the Native American and Hawaiian method of horse training.

Because she liked to draw horses and hadn't for a while, Darby sketched a surprised Hoku with wide-open eyes and long eyelashes, surging through waves. She hesitated to add herself as the rider.

In the end she didn't do it, because she didn't think tomorrow would really be the day. When she finally rode Hoku, she wanted it to be like a pact between them.

Having Kit there would be okay, but the resort . . . Darby shook her head. She just couldn't picture it.

What if guests or gardeners were watching? Darby didn't want to put Hoku through those first bewildering moments in front of an audience.

Besides, the hotel and its grounds were Duckie's home territory. Something could go wrong.

Darby wrote in her diary and added a few words

to her dictionary before she fell asleep. She roused slightly when she heard Aunty Cathy and Megan laughing, walking from Kimo's truck, passing under the candlenut tree, and climbing the staircase to their upstairs apartment.

Darby sighed and cuddled back down under her blankets. She was fast asleep by the time Jonah opened the front door and replaced the note on the kitchen table with a package from her mother.

"What will it be like, riding Hoku for the first time?" Darby asked Kit the next morning.

It wasn't as early as it had been when they'd gone to Sugar Sands yesterday, but silvery fog still veiled the island as they rolled toward the resort.

Hoku had loaded so easily in the big trailer, Darby was astounded. She couldn't guess why neither Kit nor Cade gave the filly proper admiration for it. Kit had talked more about the perfection of the newly welded hitch than the mustang.

"Getting on her for the first time, ya mean?" Kit asked as if he'd been mulling over her question.

"Yes," she said, realizing the difference with a smile. "I keep wondering if she's going to just dance around, or will she fight me? I couldn't stand that."

"I don't think you'll have to," Kit said. "She's a runner. I'm thinkin' she might try to bolt out from under you."

"That wouldn't be so bad," Darby said, because Hoku couldn't run that fast in the water.

"Just keep her headed away from the beach," Kit said.

Darby nodded as her pulse pounded hard in her wrists. She imagined leaning on her filly's salty neck, swimming out to sea.

"She won't explode like a bucking bronco?" Darby asked.

"I can't promise she won't," Kit said, "but I *can* tell you it ain't all bad when it happens."

Darby remembered Sam Forster mentioning the foreman's happy wolf smile, and she'd bet that was what she was seeing right now.

"You're a bronc rider," Darby pointed out, "and I've only been riding for a month. I'm pretty sure riding a bucking horse wouldn't be that fun for me."

"It'll be okay," Kit assured her. "It's natural to be a little anxious, a little scared, even, but it'll just make you more alert. If you treat today like an ordinary day of training, odds are Hoku will, too."

Spikes of black lava flanked the road, and Darby twisted in her seat to make sure her horse was riding as quietly as she seemed to be.

She was.

"You know, if you get out there and change your mind in trying to get on her back, there's no shame in it," Kit said.

"I know," Darby said. "I only get one first chance, and I want to get it right."

"I hear ya," Kit said, and drove on.

They'd just rolled into the corral area and parked, then waved at Babe, who was in with the cremellos, when Darby heard a shrill voice.

"Take your dog!"

Darby recognized Duckie's tone before the door on one of the resort's cottages opened.

Duckie slipped out, pushing an old dog in front of her.

"It's my Pumpkin," Babe said. She ignored Duckie and leaned forward to cluck at the dog.

He was old, gray-muzzled, and panting, even though the hotel courtyard was still covered in shade.

"He's so sweet," Darby said. He reminded her of Peach.

Wearing an oversize hot-pink sweatshirt that fell to her knees, Duckie regarded the dog with disgust.

"I agree with Phillipe." She addressed Babe, as if she hadn't noticed Darby or Kit. "That's a disgusting, smelly animal. It doesn't fit in here."

"Duxelles, Phillipe said no such thing," Babe said, pretending to tease. "He knows what Pumpkin means to me."

Duckie shrugged and walked off.

*Without telling us if she's off to get a latte or a lobotomy,* Darby thought.

"This one of Jonah's Aussies?" Kit asked as he kneaded the old dog's ears.

"He was," Babe said. "Lucky for both of them I'm the softhearted member of the family."

Darby didn't say anything, but Babe's short, sleek haircut and deft, professional attitude didn't make her seem softhearted.

"What happened?" Darby asked.

"One afternoon before our . . . falling out . . . I was afoot in the Upper Sugar Mill pasture—the cattle pasture," Babe clarified, "and Pumpkin was with me. He wasn't much more than a pup and he'd never been very cowy, but I babied him and, I admit, made him worse."

Darby shrugged her shoulders almost up to her ears. As soon as Babe noticed, she chuckled. "So you've had that lecture, too, have you? About horses, I guess?"

Darby nodded, thinking of Jonah's shout not to touch the horses on the first day they'd met.

"Anyway," Babe went on, "Pumpkin spooked a cow with long horns. They were three or four feet long, jutting straight out from her forehead. And, cows being animals of very poor judgment, she charged me." Babe's hands gestured to her ribs as she explained, "Her horns slammed me into a tree and pinned me there until she got tired of my screaming and Pumpkin's barking.

"When Jonah got to us, once he saw I was alive,

he said Pumpkin had to get off his ranch one way or the other. He's lived here ever since," Babe said.

The old dog rubbed cloudy eyes against Babe's silk dress, and the woman didn't seem to mind. In fact, she just rumpled the dog's ears.

"Shall we get this filly into the water?" Kit suggested then.

Darby rushed into a changing hut and pulled on the perfect red bathing suit her mom had sent her. Earlier that morning, she had found the package that Jonah had left for her on the kitchen table.

"Could Mom's timing be any better?" Darby asked Pumpkin, since he'd followed her.

He thumped his tail as she gathered her hair up into a ponytail—just in case she had to use it to "call" Hoku.

Next, she pulled her long-sleeved chambray shirt back on over her bathing suit. Then, carrying her jeans and slippers, Darby headed back toward Hoku.

With a twinge of surprise, she saw that for a woman who didn't believe in the family horse-charming talent, Babe was having great success with Hoku.

"Hello, *Ipo*, my sweetheart," Babe cooed to the filly, and Hoku nickered from inside the trailer. "You are a beauty, aren't you? And so friendly."

"It's just men she hates," Kit muttered.

Hoku flattened her ears at the sound of his voice, but when the back of the trailer was lowered and

Darby picked up the ten-foot lead rope, the filly turned and followed her.

"Like I told you in the truck," Kit reminded Darby, "keep her faced away from shore. Let her get used to the water before you try anything. Then, use your head."

Darby hurried, hoping no more morning joggers would hit the beach and stop to stare as one already had.

Darby felt self-conscious as she led Hoku toward the shallow waves, but she kept going.

At seven o'clock in the morning, the beach was still cool. Fog lay on the water, drifting up in skeins of white and pewter.

Chills rose on Darby's arms and legs, but they had nothing to do with the temperature.

"You've worked horses in the water before, Mr. Ely?" Babe asked.

"Yes, ma'am," Kit replied, "and if I could mention just one thing about Stormbird . . ."

"Of course," Babe said.

"Well, I been thinkin' about it since the kids brought 'im back. That colt's smart. He knows he got away once before by swimming. I'd keep him far away from the water, 'least 'til he's a yearling."

"That's a good suggestion," Babe replied, but Darby wasn't so sure she even heard, because she simply smoothed a hand over her black hair and said,

"Now let's see if my grand-niece can swim with her wild Nevada mustang."

Darby smiled, because she knew already that she could.

Leading Hoku across the sugar-white sands, into the wavelets, then deeper, until water lapped her knees, and then her hips, made Darby so breathless, she couldn't talk to her horse.

Hoku took one look at the ocean, spreading before her like a blue-gray range, and leaped.

Holding the rope with both hands, Darby got a mouthful of seawater as the filly towed her out, then under, then back to the surface.

Breathe. Swallow. Cough. Sneeze.

Darby got the order of things all mixed up, but she had an instant to rub at her nose with one hand before they were off again.

With a joyous neigh, Hoku swam on. Darby fell in beside her. Together they rose up the face of a white-veined wave, then slid down its gray back.

When they finally reached a lull, a wondrous flat place that waves left calm, Darby looked into her horse's eyes. They flashed, igniting with the thrill of going where she wanted, as fast as she wanted.

And then Hoku turned around. Her slender legs struck out and the churning currents that the horse created swirled around Darby's legs.

*Keep her headed out to sea,* Kit had told her. Far off on the beach, like a tiny model man constructed of bits of toothpick, stood Kit. She could barely see him. He must be worried that she was so far out.

Next to Kit was a dab of yellow. Babe.

Where was Duckie?

"Who knows or cares?" Darby asked Hoku, and then the filly pounced through the center of a wave as it streaked toward the shore.

Darby held on and followed.

Tail floating, mane spreading on the ocean's surface, Hoku swam openmouthed, catching satiny water on her lips, daring Darby to do the same.

Head level with Hoku's, Darby clung to the lead rope and let her legs trail behind, making kicks that were enough to propel her forward, side by side with Hoku.

They'd gone out far enough. Darby had just swung back around, heading the filly back to the beach, when she saw something.

Darby's eyes caught the flash of something pale and missile-shaped below the waves.

Was it a shark? Darby's panic telegraphed down the rope.

Hoku's head snapped right, then left. Together, they lost sight of whatever zinged along the filly's belly.

She couldn't see it, but she felt it.

Hoku launched into the air with such power that Darby, at the end of the rope, became airborne.

Chapter 17

"It's okay, Hoku. Good girl. You're fine." Darby babbled assurance to her wild filly while running her hands over the sorrel's neck, sighting down her shoulder, and bracing herself for blood billowing into the water.

So far, she saw no injuries.

Someone on the beach gave a yell of, "Ride 'em, cowgirl."

Kit motioned for her to come into shore.

Hoku trembled and even plunged her head into the water, searching for what had passed beneath her before shaking rainbow droplets that cascaded down on them both.

*We're okay,* Darby told herself as she began wondering if your face could be spanked by water. She never knew hitting the surface of a wave could feel like slamming into concrete.

Darby felt dizzy and disoriented, but Hoku was safe.

Better than that, Hoku was interested in the birds bobbing on the waves nearby.

And by Duckie.

*Duckie.*

Taking in the other girl's sleek hair and white bathing suit, Darby knew what had happened.

She and Hoku hadn't spotted a shark beneath them. They'd seen a daredevil dart between Hoku's swimming legs to touch her soft belly and make her, for just an instant, mad with fear.

"You think you're a pretty good swimmer, don't you?" Duckie said, clearing her forehead of dripping hair.

Darby whirled around to face the girl and glared.

*I think I could drown you, right here and now,* she thought.

Enraged, Darby couldn't think of anything else she wanted to say to her idiot cousin, so she turned away.

And that's when Duckie grabbed her ankle and jerked her underwater.

Surfacing, Darby saw Hoku's distended nostrils and worried eyes.

As much as she wanted to shove Duckie's head

underwater to punish her, Darby took care of her horse instead. Murmuring comforting sounds, Darby rubbed her shoulder against Hoku's neck and urged the filly to swim beside her to the shore.

Still, Duckie bellowed after them, "Take a joke, can't you?"

Hoku trotted up the beach, veering away from Kit and Babe.

The sand burned Darby's feet, and she needed both fists tight on the lead rope to control her horse.

Kit stalked alongside the sorrel, as near as he could get, as ready to help as he could be without further scaring the filly.

The cowboy looked like he had plenty to say, but he didn't speak first.

"Was that Duxelles?"

Hoku spooked and shied at Babe's voice. Darby nodded.

"I'm so sorry, Darby. She has no idea about horses."

A single glance away from her horse told Darby that Babe looked as cool and stylish as ever. But Babe's fingers were interlaced as if she were praying when she added, "I wanted to offer you free board here for your horse, instead of trailering her back and forth while you're doing water training, but I suppose that's out of the question."

"Yeah." Darby hoped her tone conveyed she

didn't blame Babe, because just then Hoku reared, shining with saltwater. Her forelegs pawed the air. They seemed almost pinned together as they rose to hide the white star on her chest.

Even when she came back to earth, the mustang rolled her eyes. She lunged from side to side, slamming against the end of her lead rope with such strength, Kit had to help Darby hold Hoku until seawater had turned to sweat and she stopped fighting out of weariness.

Finally, the filly bolted into the trailer.

"I have to talk to her," Darby said. She knew how that sounded, like she believed she could converse with her horse. But on some level Darby knew it was true.

Against his better judgment, Kit allowed her to go inside the trailer with her horse. He held the back door open and kept watch.

"You're more mad than scared, right, girl?" Darby whispered to Hoku.

The filly glared at Darby, then moved her muzzle out of reach when Darby tried to touch it.

"I took you someplace you thought was safe—and I thought it was, too—and then a scary thing happened."

Hoku blew hot breath through her nostrils. Darby was shivering and the filly's warmth comforted her. If only Hoku wasn't stamping, urging Darby to leave.

*Thank goodness I wasn't riding her when it happened,* Darby thought.

At last Hoku accepted a pat on her neck, and Darby decided that was the best time to leave.

As she walked away from her horse and down the ramp, Darby knew that Duckie's prank had fractured Hoku's trust in her. As Kit locked the tailgate, he glanced to where Babe still stood and muttered, "You are a saint. If I'd been you out there—" Kit broke off, shaking his head.

Once they climbed into the truck, he continued angrily, "Sure as sunshine, I would've taught that girl a lesson. She coulda gotten you all killed."

Still shivering, Darby couldn't think of anything to say. Kit had only driven a few yards when he stopped the truck, turned it off, and walked back toward the hotel.

What was he going to do?

Darby had no idea, but she didn't look back. She just listened as Kit Ely's spurs rang. When he came back out of the hotel, he brought along a cup of hot cocoa.

And even though it was April in Hawaii, even though the sun shone on the sand, making heat snakes waver up from its surface, Darby was freezing. She needed the warm drink, and Kit knew it.

The cowboy remained quiet as they drove, and Darby had drunk half the cup of cocoa when she managed, "Did Hoku look okay to you?"

"She's fine," Kit said. "Hoku had a grand ol' time. Rub her down good when we get her home, and look at every nook and cranny, but I've got no worries about that filly. Why, the way she came marching onto the beach, water swooshing off her—I promise, she's just mad."

"That's what I thought, too," Darby said.

Kit shook his head, and suddenly Darby saw him shut down his anger.

Just like that, he switched it off and opened up a new topic of conversation.

"I've been thinking I want a horse of my own," Kit said.

Darby was more than happy to play that game with Kit. They lived in the midst of hundreds of horses, both wild and tame, and there was a horse for every taste and task.

"That palomino gelding in the three-year-old pasture, I bet you'd get along with him," Darby said.

"No. Now, he's a nice horse, but I've got no . . . hankerin' for him. You know what I mean, like what ya see between Jonah and Luna. That's what's growin' between you and Hoku, too."

Darby nodded. Now that they'd reached the highway, the motion of the truck was as soothing as a rocking chair.

"I bet you'll pick one of the wild horses," Darby suggested, and Kit's somber face lit up.

"Ya got good instincts," Kit told her. "And yeah,

my horse is all picked out. Have you seen my brother's horse? This one kinda reminds me of her. Not in looks, but she's by golly a witch.

"I don't know what your grandfather would say—or what kinda smarts it would show, if—well, let's just put it this way. There's a limit to how many bones a man oughta be willing to break in a lifetime."

Kit drove with both hands positioned at the top of the steering wheel, and Darby would bet he didn't even notice the fingers of his right hand were rubbing his ruined left wrist.

Had he been hurt, helping her hold on to Hoku? Or did the memory of bronc-broken bones make it ache?

"Even though my contract with Jonah is just a handshake, he asked me not to rodeo while I work for him," Kit went on. "And takin' on a mustang as my pet horse might not be real different from ridin' broncs.

"I've about worn us both out with all my talk," Kit said then. "Why don't you see if you can catch a nap before we get back to the ranch."

The rest of Saturday and all day Sunday, Darby worked and read and did homework within sight of Hoku. She'd talked to everyone on the ranch, and Ann, about the filly's scare with Duckie, and everyone agreed keeping company with the mustang was the best cure.

It wasn't that Hoku had stopped liking her. The filly watched Darby attentively all the time, but it was clear that they'd lost ground.

On a hunch, Darby tucked her new red tank suit into her backpack on Monday morning. If Coach Roffmore mentioned trying out for the swim team one more time, she'd be ready to jump in.

"You look deadly," Ann told Darby as she found her seat in English and slid into it five minutes early.

"Just deadly serious," Darby said.

"Planning your revenge on Duckie?"

Darby just shrugged. Her plan wasn't exactly foolproof, so she'd better keep it to herself for now. But Ann looked so frustrated, Darby flashed her friend a smile and asked, "Hey, why don't we ever go riding together?"

"We'll have plenty of time once you get expelled," Ann told her. She waited a second. When Darby just kept smiling, Ann said, "Okay, you don't want to talk about Duckie, so here's the deal. All you've gotta do is ask me to show up on a horse and I'll be there," Ann said. "You should probably ask Jonah first, though. I have this reputation, which is only *half* true, but some people, Jonah being one of them, can't decide whether they should admire me or ban me from their property."

"Thanks for the warning," Darby said. "And, I don't think I'm going to be kicked out of school. In fact, if my plan works, Duckie and I may have a whole different relationship soon."

The first thing Darby noticed when she walked into P.E. was that Coach Day was missing. Darby wondered if her favorite teacher was talking with the dean of discipline about Duckie's accusation that Darby had tripped her.

This would be such a great school if not for Duckie. And why did they have to be related?

Darby sighed. Maybe it wasn't too late to change her class schedule. And get her DNA rewired.

But no, she thought as she double-knotted her shoelaces, her plan would work.

"Eyes on me," Coach Roffmore barked.

Darby straightened up in time to hear Duckie mutter, "Stormbird is an ugly colt. When Phillipe gets back, he'll get rid of him."

Darby tried not to answer, but she couldn't help explaining, "He'll be a big horse, and he has to grow into his ears and legs."

"Carter!"

"Sorry, Coach," she apologized.

What she really wanted to do was ask how Duckie could babble endlessly and never get caught, while she *always* did.

"Even Jan said it was good luck the colt went overboard. He looks like a gremlin or a gargoyle, or one of those things."

"If you don't want to run more laps, Carter, give me your full attention."

"I don't want to do more laps, Coach Roff-more—"

"Do you know what his new nickname is? Shark Bait. He's always wandering toward the water. Who'd know if—"

"Keep quackin', Duckie!" Darby shouted, but this time when the coach told her to run laps, she refused.

"What?" he yelled.

Darby had read about people in trouble finding the calm stillness inside themselves. For just a second, she thought she had it.

Her calm could be from lack of oxygen, because she'd been hyperventilating in fury. Or maybe she was just holding tight to the hope that she, the flea, could make big Duckie sorry she'd ever met her. Most of all, though, she realized that Duckie, without meaning to, had improved Darby's plan about 100 percent.

"I said, no, Coach. I—may I please swim laps instead of running them? For a change."

There were giggles all around her.

*I'm a good kid*, Darby thought for a second. She could not believe one girl and one little horse had turned her lifetime of perfect citizenship grades upside down.

But she shook her head. If things went the way

she hoped they would, life would start improving tomorrow.

Coach Roffmore looked surprised, and almost pleased.

"Sure, show me what you're made of, Carter," he said as he made a note on his clipboard. "Come in at lunch and you can have your own special detention."

"Coach!" The squeaky voice belonged to Selena. "Don't give up your lunch break. Just let her swim laps against us."

Another setup, Darby thought. She'd be swimming against the swim team.

"What do you say, Carter? The offer to *run* laps is still open," the Coach said, teasing her.

"Thanks, Coach," Darby said, "but I'll swim. See you after school!"

Chapter 18

The only open lane in the swimming pool was the one next to Duckie.

It was probably no accident, Darby thought as she walked out onto the concrete deck surrounding the swimming pool.

On the days she'd watched the team practice, there'd been more gossiping and giggling.

It didn't feel like a regular practice day. If the rest of the team saw her as an intruder, a bad girl who was only here for detention, would they have left a lane open for her?

*Knock it off,* Darby told herself. She was just projecting her own tension onto the others.

But then two girls she didn't recognize passed by.

One flashed her a thumbs-up and the other pretended to be speaking into a microphone as she said, "Lehua High presents the first annual Water Babies grudge match!"

Water Babies. She'd heard about a Water Babies fund-raiser on the school announcements. Was that what the team had nicknamed themselves?

She glanced over to see Duckie ease out of the water onto the pool edge. She leaned back, sunning herself.

She doesn't look like any kind of *baby*, Darby thought. With her metal-bright hair and toned muscles, she looked like an adult athlete.

Darby waited for Duckie to do something corny like draw a finger across her throat or pretend her hand was a gun and shoot it silently across the pool, like she was signing, *You're dead*.

But she didn't, and Darby knew why. The other girl was at home here. More than that, she was queen here. She didn't need to put on a milk-chugging performance to earn attention.

Duxelles Borden gazed across the dancing aqua water with total confidence. The real show would be in the pool.

Darby swallowed hard. She was doing this for Hoku, even though no one knew it yet.

She could almost hear her mother's frustrated voice say, *Does everything have to be about horses?*

*Yes, Mom,* she thought. *I guess it does!*

The concrete was hot under Darby's bare feet, but the water was cool.

She did a lazy warm-up. She didn't give the team members much to talk about, because she did nothing fancy. No butterfly or breast stroke. Those strokes took up room, and she didn't want to lift her head to look up too often.

Just often enough to avoid a head-on collision, because she'd bet Duckie's thick skull could inflict major pain.

Darby's muscles slid and reached just as she'd hoped they would. Maybe ranch work and riding counted as cross-training, she thought, smiling. Still, she felt a little lonely without Heather swimming beside her.

An ear-piercing whistle made her grab the edge of the pool and look toward the fence.

The entire girls' soccer team waved. And Coach Day stood with them, so they must be delaying practice until . . .

She jumped at the sound of Coach Roffmore's voice, but he only said, "Sync up, girls. Don't sprint while the person next to you is doing kick drills."

It sounded familiar. It even felt familiar.

*Concentrate on that,* Darby told herself, *not on the audience at the fence or on being a feisty flea set on payback.*

"When you're ready, Carter," Coach Roffmore said, "just show me what you got."

"Get 'er done, cowgirl!"

Nervous as she was, Darby smiled at Ann Potter's shout, then laughed out loud when Ann followed up with an unself-conscious "Yee haw!"

Half her tension vanished while she waited to stop laughing. A girl could drown trying to swim and laugh at the same time.

And then she was swimming.

At the wall, tight tuck, knees to chest—*yes!* Her first push-off was a monster. The instant her feet left the wall she was halfway across the pool.

*Streamline.*

It wasn't a race, and no one had scheduled a competition, but she felt Duckie swimming beside her.

*Streamline,* Darby reminded herself again, as if the pleading, demanding, promising voices of every coach she'd ever had were standing at poolside, shouting.

Hands together, shoulders against ears, eyes looking down.

But how close was Duckie? *Don't look 'til your turn. Don't lift your head like Superman going for a spin across the sky.*

*That's like putting on the brakes. Just streamline.*

For a few seconds she got that spacey feeling of seeing herself from above.

*Breathe right,* she ordered herself; but how long would they keep this up?

Whoever had been in the lane on her other side had vanished, but not Duckie.

Rhythmic as a robot, she moved down the next lane.

*I can go faster and farther,* Darby thought.

*Tight tuck. Knees to chest.*

*Jet-powered off that wall!*

*Head down, shoulders against ears—not jaw, dummy! Shoulders against ears.*

*Good form shaves off seconds. Do it right. Streeeamline.*

Darby didn't realize she was swimming blind until she made a turn and heard Coach Roffmore's whistle screeching about two inches away from her head.

She stopped, tried to put her feet down, and grasped the fact that she was in deep water only after she went under.

Then she bobbed up, made a few weak strokes to the side, and looked around.

She was the only one in the pool, but there were lots of people watching.

Darby gulped in air, then thought for the first time all day, maybe all week, about her asthma.

Her next breath tested her lungs. They passed!

Then Coach Roffmore's hand reached down to help her out of the pool.

It didn't take long for Duckie to phone.

Darby had fallen asleep on her bed before dinner.

Tired as she was, there'd been no chance to nod off in Kimo's truck when Aunty Cathy had picked up her and Megan, because Megan had been bouncing around saying, "You're number one!" and "Watch my lips, you broke the school record and Duxelles's all-time record."

"Record for what?" Darby had managed. "It must be her best time. It couldn't be distance."

"I don't know! I just heard him click his stopwatch like you were a racehorse he was timing, and say, 'By George, that's a record.'" Then Megan had leaned forward from the backseat and asked, "Mom, Coach Roffmore isn't English, is he? Doesn't that sound kind of—"

"I have no idea." Aunty Cathy had laughed, then turned to Darby and asked, "So are you going to do it? Join the swim team?"

"No—"

"Of course you are! You have to!" Megan insisted.

But Darby crossed her fingers, yawned, and hoped she wouldn't have to.

Darby didn't really have much idea how she'd gotten inside, on her bed, but now Jonah was bellowing from her bedroom doorway.

"You, Sleeping Beauty," he said, smiling. "You got a call from your cousin."

The bed seemed too soft to push off of, but Darby managed to get to her feet.

"Thanks," she said, wobbling down the hallway.

Before he let her pass, Jonah joked, "Then dinner

on the lanai, with your fans, you little record-breaker, you."

"So, are you going to change your mind and join the team?" Duckie demanded before Darby finished saying hello.

"I told you I didn't have time," Darby said. Collapsing into a chair at the kitchen table, she smothered a yawn, but kept the phone to her ear.

"Roffmore practically kissed your feet."

It was true, Darby thought. The same man who'd picked on her since she'd walked into his P.E. class had actually said he'd quit coaching if she didn't join.

"He exaggerated about how well I did. You know that."

Darby looked up. Megan had come to lean against one side of the kitchen doorway, openly eavesdropping.

When Duckie stayed quiet, Darby reviewed what she'd just said and knew that hadn't been right. It kind of implied that Duckie wasn't that great.

Wincing, Darby said, "Besides, you almost killed me. I'll never be able to swim that way again, and then he'll be so disappointed, he'll think I'm useless."

Megan caught Darby's eye and pantomimed putting her finger down her throat.

Darby turned away.

"So you're really, honestly, not going to join?" Duckie asked.

Apparently Duckie believed everyone was as sneaky as she was. She still wasn't convinced.

And that, Darby thought with a sly smile, was what she and Heather used to call a V.G.T., a Very Good Thing.

"No, I swear I won't join the team, if . . ." Darby paused. She rolled her eyes up and counted the whitewashed boards in the ceiling.

"If?" Duckie demanded.

"Well . . ." Darby stretched out her cousin's torture. "I won't, if you help me with something."

After she'd explained, Duckie had still been unconvinced that there wasn't more to Darby's promise not to join the team, but she agreed to meet her early Saturday morning at the Sugar Sands Cove beach.

When Darby hung up, she was yawning again and trying to put her soggy ponytail into some kind of order. Megan looked at her with something like suspicion mingled with respect.

"What?" Darby asked. "I forgot something? Is she going to ambush me and beat me up?"

Of course it had been too easy. What kind of dumb mistake had she made?

"I don't think so," Megan said. "It's just that you're getting so good at being bad, you'd better watch yourself. Especially if you're going to hang around with Annie Potter."

❊ ❊ ❊

Jonah was so glad to have his Land Rover fixed that he volunteered to take Hoku and Darby to Sugar Sands Cove Resort for their second water training.

She didn't ask him how the window had been broken. She was just happy they had two vehicles again, and glad Jonah wasn't so dead-set against Babe's "dude" idea that he refused to go near his sister and her cremellos.

As suspicious as Hoku had been of Darby since Duxelles had sabotaged their first water-training attempt, she loaded just as easily as before into the trailer.

"You did a good job working with her. She loads real nice," Jonah said as he locked the back of the horse trailer.

"But I didn't," Darby said. "She just does it naturally."

"Hmm. Well, I guess it could have to do with Cathy."

"Aunty Cathy?"

"Seems like I saw her putting chunks of apple in an aluminum bowl and carrying it out here, putting it in the trailer."

Amazed, Darby stared at him. Did he mean it smelled good in there, so Hoku didn't mind going in?

"Yeah," Jonah said, nodding. "Then it seems like your little horse got curious, walked up close, and stretched her neck out like a giraffe, then used her lips to grab that bowl. She just started pulling it toward herself when your aunty Cathy—yeah, I'm pretty sure it was her—said, "Oh no, you don't. If you want to eat them, you have to do it inside the trailer.'"

"Wow!" Darby said. "When did she do all this?"

"Hard to remember," Jonah said, stroking a knuckle over his mustache and squinting. "Coulda been while you were at school."

It would have been too sappy to say that every day she felt more at home on 'Iolani Ranch, but it was true.

"That is so cool," Darby said as they pulled out of the ranch yard. "I'll thank her as soon as we get back home."

Jonah gave a satisfied nod.

They'd turned onto the main highway when Jonah said, "I like this solution of yours."

"Oh, good," Darby said. "I hope it works."

"Gotta try it and see," Jonah said. "Only way."

"Yep," she agreed.

"Just like my truck."

*Oh, no.* Darby felt a sudden flash of worry. Jonah hadn't done one of his random story sessions for a while, but she hadn't missed them. They usually left her feeling like she'd missed half of what he was trying to tell her.

And if this story involved truck parts, she didn't see how her grandfather would expect her to get it.

"When the Land Rover didn't start, I tried jump-starting it off Kimo's Ram."

Darby nodded. She wasn't exactly sure what jump-starting was, but she thought it might have been that thing he and Kimo did when they ran cables between the two trucks.

"That didn't work, so I replaced the battery. That didn't work, either, but when I disconnected the battery, this truck locked me inside."

"I did everything myself," Jonah pointed out.

"I noticed," Darby said.

She glanced at the broken back window. She'd bet Jonah had had a cell phone in his pocket and had been too stubborn to use it, but she didn't ask.

"But I finally got it going. See, there was one cable that looked good, but it wasn't. I didn't know 'til I tested it."

"Yep," Darby said, but she was thinking that Kit must be a faster driver than Jonah.

"Like you," Jonah said.

"Yeah?"

"You tried being nice. Then you had to get mean back at your cousin."

"Well, she —"

Jonah held his palm out, stopping her.

"It didn't work, but hey, that's how it goes sometimes. Then, you beat her at her own game and *didn't* rub her face in it." He gave Darby's shoulder a gentle shove. "I call that success."

Darby saw the sparkling sugar-white buildings of the resort ahead and hoped her grandfather would have another reason to admire her on their way home.

Her plan was simple.

Darby had decided that she'd teach Hoku that *people* in the water — especially Duckie — were nothing to fear.

She planned to reenact the day she'd gone swimming with Hoku as closely as she could. She wouldn't try to ride her. She'd just swim with her and, sometime, Duckie would swim beneath her.

Before tourists began strolling the beach and before she unloaded Hoku, Darby went over everything with her cousin.

"Are you sure this is going to work?" Duckie looked cranky. She'd told Darby she did not get up this early on weekends.

Strangely, without her anger to cloud her judgment, she'd realized swimming among a horse's hooves could be dangerous.

"Horses are natural swimmers and they like it. The only reason she got panicky, there at the end, was because you scared her."

Duckie put her hands on the hips of her white bathing suit, implying there was no way she'd apologize.

"I don't want you to say you're sorry," Darby told her. "Just help me teach her she's okay out there."

Darby stared out at the ocean. "Usually. Oh, and make sure she sees you coming before you go diving near her."

"And if I do this, I've got the Water Babies all to myself again?"

It was a weird way to put her swimming-star status, but Darby said, "Right, but I'm also assuming that you said that awful stuff about Stormbird not because you'd really hurt him but—"

"Just to make you mad, so you'd get in trouble with Coach."

"Okay," Darby said.

The sun sent streamers of light through the clouds as Darby led Hoku toward the ocean.

Alert and cautious, Hoku held each hoof up for an extra second before she set it down. She raised her head high, sighting over the waves, but every few steps she'd lower her chin to graze the top of Darby's head.

They were still in shallow water, but directly out from where Duckie had pulled her "prank," when Hoku made a clacking sound with her teeth.

"Poor baby," Darby said, stroking the filly's neck.

She'd read that when horses did that, it was a submissive gesture. It meant, *Please don't hurt me; I'm just a baby.*

"I won't let anyone hurt you, Hoku."

"Stop hugging," Jonah called from the shore.

His timing was perfect. Hoku gave up fear to turn

her flat-eared glare on the interfering male. Then she strode on, beside Darby.

"Give her plenty of rope when you get out there, yeah?" Jonah yelled.

Darby turned, cupping her hand at her ear so that he'd speak up over the waves.

"She's gonna need her head and neck free. Some guy in the Caribbean drowned his horse, riding with a tie-down or martingale or one of those things. Dumb. Horse shoulda taken the guy with him."

Darby waved a sign that she'd gotten the point of the story, and kept walking.

When they were chest deep, Hoku recognized the sea she'd enjoyed before.

She gave a long neigh, as if this was a window to the world she'd known before, a range that just happened to have waves instead of sagebrush.

She began swimming, hardly noticing when Darby let go of the lead rope and clung to Hoku's mane instead.

Darby floated. Swept along by Hoku's motion, Darby's swim-strained muscles didn't work at all. She glided through satiny waves as Hoku stretched out in a streamlined position of her own.

Then Hoku gave a snort, and Darby noticed that the filly's attention was focused on movement farther out.

Somehow Duckie had gotten ahead of them.

She was saying something. Or . . . singing?

As Duckie drew closer, Darby realized her cousin was imitating the "shark music" from the old movie *Jaws*.

"Not funny," Darby said. But it was, just a little bit.

For someone who claimed to have zero interest in horses, Duckie had good instincts, Darby thought.

Her cousin swam a huge circle around Darby and Hoku, decreasing its size so gradually that at first Darby didn't notice.

Then, as she came closer, Duckie swam underwater, but she kept a hand visible—raised at first, then trailed atop the sea.

"Good job," Darby said softly, and Hoku must have thought the appreciation was for her, because she slowed long enough to nibble the shoulder strap of Darby's new red tank suit.

The pause was enough to make the sorrel's body dip in the water. Blinking, Hoku seemed to understand that no shore underfoot meant she had to keep moving.

As decisively as if she and Darby had discussed it, Hoku swam in an arc. Her powerful strokes raised a swell of water that washed over Darby. The mustang was headed back toward the beach.

Duckie must not have realized how preoccupied the filly was with her return to solid earth, because she picked that moment to zip toward Hoku, underwater.

"Here she comes, girl," Darby warned.

She pointed, as if Hoku would follow her gesture. It didn't make sense that she would, because it didn't fall into any of the horse communication categories Darby could think of, but she did it anyway.

Hoku's water trot slowed and her head and neck swung toward the white object arrowing toward them.

"It's just Duckie," Darby said in a teasing tone, but Hoku arched her neck and fixed her eyes on the thing.

If the tension in the filly's body was equal to her concentration, Hoku was trying to figure out whether this white thing matched with the one that had been humming and swimming circles around her.

Duckie swam past about six feet away from them, then turned around and came back closer.

Darby couldn't tell if her mustang was trembling from fear or anticipation, but when Duckie skimmed up close to the horse's belly, where Darby couldn't even see her, she found out it was neither.

It was curiosity.

Hoku plunged her head and neck underwater, dragging Darby along with her.

Darby opened her eyes. For a few seconds, she stared, as Hoku did. A blue-green world surrounded a glowing figure.

"It was just Duckie," she told Hoku as they lifted their heads.

Hoku snorted. She shook her mane. Darby just

dodged the horse's heavy, wet head before Hoku thrust it underwater again.

This time Darby didn't go with her.

The filly blew bubbles through her mouth and nose, and when Darby jerked at the lead rope, afraid something was wrong, Hoku only grudgingly came back up.

"Doesn't that sting—"

Hoku snorted saltwater in Darby's face. Once more she brandished her slippery head like a weapon and Darby was lucky to get out of the way.

"I've had enough fun," Darby said, laughing at the horse.

Hoku seemed to understand, because she struck out for the beach, towing Darby right beside her.

Jonah and Duckie were waiting, about ten feet apart, when Darby and Hoku came ashore.

Hoku shook again, splattering them all with salt-water, then gave a satisfied nicker.

"She's not glaring at you," Darby said to Jonah, but he didn't get as excited as she was.

"Get water up her nose?" he asked, nodding back out at the sea.

"Yeah," Darby said, laughing. "But she didn't seem to mind much."

"Lead her around some," he said. "I'm gonna take a look at those weak-eyed cremello horses of my sister's so she'll leave me in peace."

Darby didn't see Aunt Babe anywhere around,

but she said, "Okay," and began walking Hoku, cooling her out as if she'd just had a long run.

To Darby's surprise, Duckie walked beside them for a minute.

"It's okay if you call me Duckie," she said. "It's not like it's some major secret, but I hate you doing it behind my back. Since it kind of goes with my swimming, I like it better than my other nicknames."

"Okay," Darby said, but she was talking to her cousin's back, because Duckie was already walking away.

Then she turned back, hands on hips, and said, "Just don't think this means we're friends, though."

"Okay," Darby said again.

Duckie seemed to regret being civil, because she added, "If you go changing your mind about the swim team, I'll make your life miserable. Count on it."

And then, appearing more satisfied, Duckie strode across the beach toward the resort building.

Hoku flipped her wet forelock away from her eyes and nudged Darby.

The filly's eyes danced with sunlight reflections, and if a horse could laugh, Darby thought, hers was.

She looked around quickly for Jonah, and when she didn't see him, she circled Hoku's neck with a hug.

"This is the only swim team I want to be on. I pick you, Hoku. Always."

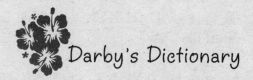 Darby's Dictionary

In case anybody reads this besides me, which it's too late to tell you not to do if you've gotten this far, I know this isn't a real dictionary. For one thing, it's not all correct, and for another, it's not alphabetized because I'm just adding things as I hear them. Besides, this dictionary is just to help me remember. Even though I'm pretty self-conscious about pronouncing Hawaiian words, it seems to me if I live here (and since I'm part Hawaiian), I should at least try to say things right.

'aumakua — OW MA KOO AH — these are family guardians from ancient times. I think ancestors are supposed to come back and look out for their family members. Our 'aumakua are owls and Megan's is a sea turtle.

chicken skin — goose bumps

da kine — DAH KYNE — "that sort of thing" or "stuff like that"

hanai — HA NYE E — a foster or adopted child, like Cade is Jonah's, but I don't know if it's permanent

'iolani — EE OH LAWN EE — this is a hawk that brings messages from the gods, but Jonah has it painted on his trucks as an owl bursting through the clouds

hiapo — HIGH AH PO — a firstborn child, like me, and it's apparently tradition for grandparents, if they feel like it, to just take hiapo to raise!

hoku — HO COO — star

ali'i — AH LEE EE — royalty, but it includes chiefs besides queens and kings and people like that

pupule — POO POO LAY — crazy

paniolo — PAW KNEE OH LOW — cowboy or cowgirl

lanai — LAH NA E — this is like a balcony or veranda. Sun House's is more like a long balcony with a view of the pastures.

lei niho palaoa — LAY NEEHO PAH LAHOAH — necklace made for old-time Hawaiian royalty from braids of their own hair. It's totally kapu—forbidden—for anyone else to wear it.

luna — LOU NUH — a boss or top guy, like Jonah's stallion

pueo — POO AY OH — an owl, our family guardian. The very coolest thing is that one lives in the tree next to Hoku's corral.

pau — POW — finished, like Kimo is always asking, "You pau?" to see if I'm done working with Hoku or shoveling up after the horses

pali — PAW LEE — cliffs

ohia — OH HE UH — a tree like the one next to Hoku's corral

<u>lei</u> — LAY E — necklace of flowers. I thought they were pronounced LAY, but Hawaiians add another sound. I also thought leis were sappy touristy things, but getting one is a real honor, from the right people.

<u>lau hala</u> — LA OO HA LA — some kind of leaf in shades of brown, used to make paniolo hats like Cade's. I guess they're really expensive.

<u>kapu</u> — KAH POO — forbidden, a taboo

<u>tutu</u> — TOO TOO — great-grandmother

<u>menehune</u> — MEN AY WHO NAY — little people

<u>honu</u> — HO NEW — sea turtle

<u>hewa-hewa</u> — HEE VAH HEE VAH — crazy

<u>ipo</u> — EE POE — sweetheart, actually short for "ku'uipo"

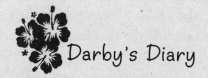 Darby's Diary

<u>Ellen Kealoha Carter</u>—my mom, and since she's responsible for me being in Hawaii, I'm putting her first. Also I miss her. My mom is a beautiful and talented actress, but she hasn't had her big break yet. Her job in Tahiti might be it, which is sort of ironic because she's playing a Hawaiian for the first time and she swore she'd never return to Hawaii. And here I am. I get the feeling she had huge fights with her dad, Jonah, but she doesn't hate Hawaii.

<u>Cade</u>—fifteen or so, he's Jonah's adopted son. Jonah's been teaching him all about being a paniolo. I thought he was Hawaiian, but when he took off his hat he had blond hair—in a braid! Like old-time

vaqueros—weird! He doesn't go to school, just takes his classes by correspondence through the mail. He wears this poncho that's almost black it's such a dark green, and he blends in with the forest. Kind of creepy the way he just appears out there. Not counting Kit, Cade might be the best rider on the ranch.

Hoku kicked him in the chest. I wish she hadn't. He told me that his stepfather beat him all the time.

Cathy Kato—forty or so? She's the ranch manager and, really, the only one who seems to manage Jonah. She's Megan's mom and the widow of a paniolo, Ben. She has messy blond-brown hair to her chin, and she's a good cook, but she doesn't think so. It's like she's just pulling herself back together after Ben's death.

I get the feeling she used to do something with advertising or public relations on the mainland.

Jonah Kaniela Kealoha—my grandfather could fill this whole notebook. Basically, though, he's harsh/nice, serious/funny, full of legends and stories about magic, but real down-to-earth. He's amazing with horses, which is why they call him the Horse Charmer. He's not that tall, maybe 5'8", with black hair that's getting gray, and one of his fingers is still kinked where it was broken by a teacher because he spoke Hawaiian in class! I don't like his "don't touch the horses unless they're working for you" theory, but it totally works. I need to figure out why.

<u>Kimo</u>—he's so nice! I guess he's about twenty-five, Hawaiian, and he's just this sturdy, square, friendly guy. He drives in every morning from his house over by Crimson Vale, and even though he's late a lot, I've never seen anyone work so hard.

<u>Kit Ely</u>—the ranch foreman, the boss, next to Jonah. He's Sam's friend Jake's brother and a real buckaroo. He's about 5'10" with black hair. He's half Shoshone, but he could be mistaken for Hawaiian, if he wasn't always promising to whip up a batch of Nevada chili and stuff like that. And he wears a totally un-Hawaiian leather string with brown-streaked turquoise stones around his neck. He got to be foreman through his rodeo friend Pani (Ben's buddy). Kit's left wrist got pulverized in a rodeo fall. He's still amazing with horses, though.

<u>Megan Kato</u>—Cathy's fifteen-year-old daughter, a super athlete with long reddish-black hair. She's beautiful and popular and I doubt she'd be my friend if we just met at school. Maybe, though, because she's nice at heart. She half makes fun of Hawaiian legends, then turns around and acts really serious about them. Her Hawaiian name is Mekana.

<u>The Zinks</u>—they live on the land next to Jonah. They have barbed-wire fences and their name doesn't sound Hawaiian, but that's all I know.

<u>Tutu</u>—my great-grandmother. She lives out in the rain forest like a medicine woman or something, and she looks like my mom will when she's old. She has a pet owl.

<u>Aunt Babe Borden</u>—Jonah's sister, so she's really my great-aunt. She owns half of the family land, which is divided by a border that runs between the Two Sisters. Aunt Babe and Jonah don't get along, and though she's fashionable and caters to rich people at her resort, she and her brother are identically stubborn. Aunt Babe pretends to be all business, but she loves her cremello horses and I think she likes having me and Hoku around.

<u>Duxelles Borden</u>—if you lined up all the people on Hawaii and asked me to pick out one NOT related to me, it would be Duxelles, but it turns out she's my cousin. Tall (I come up to her shoulders), strong, and with this metallic blond hair, she's popular despite being a bully. She lives with Aunt Babe while her mom travels with her dad, who's a world-class kayaker. About the only thing Duxelles and I have in common is we're both swimmers. Oh, and I gave her a nickname—Duckie.

## ✤ ANIMALS! ✤

<u>Hoku</u>—my wonderful sorrel filly! She's about two and a half years old, a full sister to the Phantom, and boy, does she show it! She's fierce (hates men) but smart, and a one-girl (ME!) horse for sure. She is definitely a herd-girl, and when it comes to choosing between me and other horses, it's a real toss-up. Not that I blame her. She's run free for a long time, and I don't want to take away what makes her special.

She loves hay, but she's really HEAD-SHY due to Shan Stonerow's early "training," which, according to Sam, was beating her.

*Hoku* means "star." Her dam is Princess Kitty, but her sire is a mustang named Smoke and he's mustang all the way back to a "white renegade with murder in his eye" (Mrs. Allen).

<u>Navigator</u>—my riding horse is a big, heavy Quarter Horse that reminds me of a knight's charger. He has Three Bars breeding (that's a big deal), but when he picked me, Jonah let him keep me! He's black with rusty rings around his eyes and a rusty muzzle. (Even though he looks black, the proper description is brown, they tell me.) He can find his way home from any place on the island. He's sweet, but no pushover. Just when I think he's sort of a safety net for my beginning riding skills, he tests me.

Joker—Cade's Appaloosa gelding is gray splattered with black spots and has a black mane and tail. He climbs like a mountain goat and always looks like he's having a good time. I think he and Cade have a history, maybe Jonah took them in together?

Biscuit—buckskin gelding, one of Ben's horses, a dependable cowpony. Kit rides him a lot.

Hula Girl—chestnut cutter

Blue Ginger—blue roan mare with tan foal

Honolulu Lulu—bay mare

Tail Afire (Koko)—fudge brown mare with silver mane and tail

Blue Moon—Blue Ginger's baby

Moonfire—Tail Afire's baby

Black Cat—Lady Wong's black foal

Luna Dancer—Hula Girl's bay baby

Honolulu Half Moon

Conch—grulla cowpony, gelding, needs work. Megan rides him sometimes.

Kona—big gray, Jonah's cow horse

Luna—beautiful, full-maned bay stallion is king of 'Iolani Ranch. He and Jonah seem to have a bond.

Lady Wong—dappled gray mare and Kona's dam. Her current foal is Black Cat.

Australian shepherds—pack of five: Bart, Jack, Jill, Peach, and Sass

Pipsqueak/Pip—little, shaggy, white dog that runs with the big dogs, belongs to Megan and Cathy

Tango—Megan's once-wild rose roan mare. I think she and Hoku are going to be pals.

Flight—this cremello mare belongs to Aunt Babe (she has a whole herd of cremellos) and nearly died of longing for her foal. She was a totally different horse—beautiful and spirited—once she got him back!

Stormbird—Flight's cream-colored (with a blush of palomino) foal with turquoise eyes has had an exciting life for a four-month-old. He's been ship-wrecked, washed ashore, fended for himself, and rescued.

❧ PLACES ❧

Lehua High School—the school Megan and I go to. School colors are red and gold.

Crimson Vale—it's an amazing and magical place, and once I learn my way around, I bet I'll love it. It's like a maze, though. Here's what I know: From town you can go through the valley or take the ridge road—valley has lily pads, waterfalls, wild horses, and rainbows. The ridge route (Pali?) has sweeping turns that almost made me sick. There are black rock teeter-totter-looking things that are really ancient altars and a SUDDEN drop-off down to a white sand beach. Hawaiian royalty are supposedly buried in the cliffs.

Moku Lio Hihiu—Wild Horse Island, of course!

Mountain to the Sky—sometimes just called Sky Mountain. Goes up to 5,000 feet, sometimes gets snow, and Megan said there used to be wild horses there.

<u>The Two Sisters</u>—cone-shaped "mountains." A borderline between them divides Jonah's land from his sister's—my great-aunt Babe. One of them is an active volcano. Kind of scary.

<u>Sun House</u>—our family place. They call it plantation style, but it's like sugar plantation, not Southern mansion. It has an incredible lanai that overlooks pastures all the way to Mountain to the Sky and Two Sisters. Upstairs is this little apartment Jonah built for my mom, but she's never lived in it.

<u>Hapuna</u>—biggest town on island, has airport, flagpole, public and private schools, etc., palm trees, and coconut trees

<u>'Iolani Ranch</u>—our home ranch. 2,000 acres, the most beautiful place in the world.

<u>Sugar Sands Cove Resort</u>—Aunt Babe and her polo-player husband, Phillipe, own this resort on the island. It has sparkling white buildings and beaches and a four-star hotel. The most important thing to me is that Sugar Sands Cove Resort has the perfect water-schooling beach for me and Hoku.

Sugar Mill and Upper Sugar Mill—for cattle

Two Sisters—for young horses, one- and two-year-olds they pretty much leave alone

Flatland—mares and foals

Pearl Pasture—borders the rain forest, mostly two- and three-year-olds in training

Borderlands—saddle herd and Luna's compound


I guess I should also add me . . .

Darby Leilani Kealoha Carter—I love horses more than anything, but books come in second. I'm thirteen, and one-quarter Hawaiian, with blue eyes and black hair down to about the middle of my back. On a good day, my hair is my best feature. I'm still kind of skinny, but I don't look as sickly as I did before I moved here. I think Hawaii's curing my asthma. Fingers crossed.

I have no idea what I did to land on Wild Horse Island, but I want to stay here forever.

*Darby and Hoku's adventures continue in . . .*

# FIRE MAIDEN

# Fire Maiden

"My foreman tells me Hoku is about ready to start carrying a rider," Jonah said as Darby Carter climbed out of the 'Iolani Ranch truck after school.

Darby took in everything around her. It looked just like it had when she'd left for school that morning.

She was still in Hawaii, on Wild Horse Island. The Australian shepherds were barking a welcome, and Sun House—in which she had a bedroom—was still cantilevered over a bluff, looking down on hundreds of emerald acres that made 'Iolani Ranch heaven for horses.

Across the yard, in one direction, sat the round pen.

Past it, right where it should be, was the green foreman's house next to the tack shed. Beyond that, a clutter of grayed wooden fox cages sat in the shade of a tree that often provided a hunting perch for a friendly owl. And right on down the path, she could see the corral where her filly Hoku was penned, getting used to the sights, sounds, and smells of ranch life until she was . . .

"Kit said Hoku's ready to carry a rider?" Darby finally said, then gasped.

"It's not April Fool's Day, Granddaughter," Jonah told her. "He said she did fine in the waves over at Sugar Sands and he doesn't think we should waste her curiosity."

"Wow," Darby said.

Jonah looked like he was holding in a smile.

As Megan Kato, Darby's best friend on the ranch, slid down from the truck carrying her soccer bag, she gave Darby a thumbs-up.

"Go change your clothes and meet Kit at Hoku's corral," Jonah said.

Megan flashed Darby an excited look and said, "This is so cool. I'm coming over there to watch."

"Hurry," Jonah urged, as if Darby had settled in for a chat instead of shivering with anticipation. Then he glanced at the horizon and added, "This might use up all the daylight we've got left."

Was Jonah forgetting that she and Hoku had an unpredictable relationship? Most of the time, they were sisters. Once in a while, though, the mustang filly regarded Darby with the same impatience she had for other clumsy two-legged humans.

With raised eyebrows, Darby looked at Aunty Cathy. Although Cathy Kato was Megan's mom and the ranch manager, and not really related to Darby, the woman was a respected friend that Darby honored in the Hawaiian way by calling her aunty. Besides, Cathy was an experienced horsewoman and Darby always welcomed her advice.

Pushing her brown-blond hair out of her eyes with the back of her wrist and balancing a bag of groceries on her hip, Aunty Cathy said, "I wouldn't count on teaching an untrained horse to carry a rider before dinnertime, but that's just me."

"Hmph," Jonah said. "Probably right. That filly's got too much wild horse in her. She'll just run off instead of standing and thinking like her dam."

Hoku's dam was Princess Kitty, a running Quarter Horse related to the champion Three Bars. Jonah believed Quarter Horses were royalty in the world of equines.

Jonah gave an approving nod for his own wisdom, then walked away before Darby could speak up for Hoku's mustang bloodlines.

In a mock-Western accent, Megan drawled, "Ya got 'til sundown, Horse Charmer."

"I really want to do this, but a little warning would have been nice," Darby muttered as she looked after her grandfather.

"Tell him you want to wait," Cathy suggested. "At

least until after your camping trip."

Darby's sensible side, the part of her that had ruled her life when she lived in Pacific Pinnacles, California, agreed with Aunty Cathy. She'd only been riding for a month, after all.

But Darby's Hawaiian heart, the part of her that had come to life on Wild Horse Island, overruled her head.

"No way!" Darby said, and she ran inside Sun House, down the hall to her bedroom, to pull on riding clothes.

Ten minutes later, Darby was jogging toward Kit Ely. The ranch foreman, a half-Shoshone Nevadan who was often mistaken for a Hawaiian, stood at the fence of Hoku's corral. In his customary chaps and pressed shirt, Kit looked younger than usual as he gave Darby his happy wolf smile.

*This is going to be fun,* Darby thought, and just then, her horse moved out from behind Kit.

Ears pricked at the sound of Darby's approach, the sorrel filly tossed her flaxen forelock from her eyes. Her hooves made a staccato beat as background to her snorts and nickers.

*She's glad to see me, but she wants Kit to go away.* Because the filly had been beaten by a man during her colthood, Hoku had good reasons to dislike men, but she tolerated Kit better than other males.

"Hi!" Darby heard her own singing tone as she approached.

Kit's smile showed white against his dark features. He looked almost as excited as she felt.

"This is just the beginnin'," he cautioned Darby. "Just preparation for the main event, okay?"

"Okay," Darby said, smooching at Hoku.

The sorrel stopped. She flung her muzzle toward her back, as if urging Darby to come inside the pen.

"Listen up, now," Kit said, more seriously than before.

Darby let the smile fade from her lips. Crossing her arms to keep in her exhilaration, Darby faced him.

"All we're going to do today is show her how it's done. Riding, that is," Kit said. "Together, we're going to lead her into the round pen and turn her loose, wearing just her halter. Next, you'll go inside, leading Navigator, and I'll bring you your gear and you'll tack him up."

"What will she do?"

"With luck, she'll be watching, feeling just a little jealous."

"Okay," Darby said, and she felt her smile creeping back again.

"Then you'll walk away from Navigator, leaving him ground-tied, and come talk to me. At that point, we hope she'll mosey over to sniff out the dress-up outfit her human has put on another horse. Then you'll get on him and ride around."

Darby's crazy heartbeat began to slow down.

It was enough of a challenge that it probably

would take all afternoon and early evening. But the way Jonah had greeted her, well, she'd thought that someone had swung a magic wand over Hoku's golden back, making her instantly rideable. Of course, such a thing could never happen. The wild filly trusted Darby. For now, that was the best she could hope for.

"It's a small step," Kit admitted, "but tomorrow we'll move on. We're buildin' on all you two been puttin' into each other since you met. Got it?"

"Got it!" Darby said, and she was thinking each step would go faster than Kit thought it would, because no one but her knew of the day in the rain-forest corral when Hoku had practically asked Darby to climb on and ride.

She hadn't done it that day because she would have been alone if something had gone wrong.

Now, she had Jonah's approval and Kit's supervision. She wasn't going to waste a minute.

Darby grabbed the tangerine-and-white-striped lead rope that Kit had placed over the fence. Hoku's halter was clipped onto it and the headstall was unbuckled.

As she slid back the gate's bolt to enter Hoku's corral, she noticed that Kit was holding a coiled rope. Hoku noticed, too.

Prancing with high-held knees, the filly peered over the fence and gave a doubtful snort.

Darby clucked her tongue. Hoku ran a single lap

around her corral, swinging her head from side to side like a wild stallion, then slid to a cow-pony stop in front of Darby.

"Yeah, you really scared me, didn't you?" Darby smiled. The filly's brown eyes glittered with mischief. "You're just playful because I've been at school instead of giving you my undivided attention, huh, baby?"

Holding the halter open with both hands, she approached Hoku. The filly glanced at Kit, but then took a step forward to meet Darby, and lowered her head. A little.

Darby had to stand on tiptoe to fasten the halter buckle, but Hoku's quick breaths told her the filly was eager to do something.

"Both hands on the rope," Kit said. "One up near her chin and the other about halfway down."

"I know," Darby said.

"I know you do, but she's pretty keyed up. If she decides to take off, she's gotta know you're going to act like an anchor."

Darby nodded, and Kit waited until she and Hoku had cleared the gate before coming toward her with his rope.

A wind carrying the scents of cinnamon-red dirt, lush grass, and stream-wet rocks blew toward them, and Hoku breathed man-smell in with the others.

Hoku flattened her ears for a full minute, but Kit came no closer until the filly noticed—at the same time Darby did—that Kit was singing. Darby couldn't make out the words, but the foreman sung in a minor key.

The melody was oddly familiar, and reminded Darby of a flute song meant to hypnotize cobras.

Hoku wasn't hypnotized, but as soon as her ears pricked up with curiosity, Kit moved in to snap on his rope. The filly allowed it, sniffing at the leather fringe on his chinks before pawing impatiently, telling Kit that he'd better move away from her, out to the very end of the rope. Soon.

Kit did exactly that, then matched his steps to Darby's.

The filly walked between them, neighing at Navigator as they passed. The dark gelding with rust-colored hair around his eyes was tied to a ring by the tack shed.

Though it only took the three of them a few minutes to walk uphill to the round pen, Darby felt hot and sweaty. The air was humid, but the breeze had stopped. She lifted her shoulder to wipe off a bead of sweat that had dropped from her brow to her cheek.

Hoku kept looking back at Navigator and calling to him.

"She knows today's different," Darby said quietly.

"Mustangs are smart," Kit agreed.

Darby smiled in agreement. She was so glad Kit felt that way. And he was from Nevada, where most of the world's wild horses lived, so he was an expert.

Not that it changed Jonah's opinion.

Even though her grandfather lectured everyone about the wisdom of saddle horses keeping their wild edge, so that they could think for themselves, he didn't believe mustangs like Hoku were particularly intelligent.

Jonah would stake his life on his conviction that Quarter Horses were the Einsteins of the equine world.

"I'm gonna run ahead and open the gate. You got her?" Kit asked.

"Sure."

As soon as Kit dropped his end of the rope, Hoku edged toward Darby, and then she eased into a jog, head lifted.

Darby trotted alongside her, keeping up as she teased, "Are you glad he's gone, you bad girl?"

Hoku blew her warm breath toward Darby.

Once Kit had the gate open, he returned to help Darby lead the filly through.

Hoku rolled her eyes as if something about him had frightened her. As soon as Kit picked up his end of the rope, the filly rose in a half rear, jerking up all the slack.

"Oh, no!" Darby had hoped Hoku would stay calm and playful, despite the hot, still weather and the break in her routine.

"Don't worry." Kit dodged the filly's flailing hooves as if she were a kitten. "Once we unsnap these ropes, she's gonna forget this part. She'll see you comin' in, leadin' Navigator, fussin' with Navigator, and she's gonna think that's what upset her. She'll come sniffing around to see why you're leaving her out."

Kit's prediction came pretty close.

Megan and Aunty Cathy were watching, arms crossed atop the fence, as Darby tried to saddle Navigator while Hoku interfered.

When Darby worked on the gelding's left side, Hoku approached from his right. She sniffed his nose and Navigator sniffed hers. Hoku nuzzled the gelding's sleek coffee-colored neck, and his lips brushed her golden mane.

Hoku breathed in the scent of the saddle blanket, but kept moving alongside Navigator. She stayed close enough that he began scratching her back with short, firm bites.

Darby stood holding the heavy Western saddle, poised to fling it on, when Hoku's teeth closed on the saddle blanket, slid it off the gelding's back, and proceeded to groom the gelding with short, firm bites of her own.

Although she heard Aunty Cathy and Megan laughing, Darby held her amusement in, because she saw Jonah approaching and he didn't look pleased.

"Shhhhhoo!" Darby hissed at Hoku. The snaky sound was one the filly didn't like, and she moved off in time for Darby to put down the saddle, replace the blanket, and swing the saddle onto Navigator's back before Jonah entered the corral.

Hoku squealed a "how dare you" reprimand at Jonah when he slid the bolt closed behind himself and stood talking to Kit.

"Go ahead and mount up," Kit called to Darby.

She did, but she was aware of Hoku aiming betrayed snorts her way.

For a long time, probably twenty minutes, Hoku stood with her tail turned toward Darby and Navigator as Darby rode the gelding at a walk, jog, and lope.

Once, as Darby rode past, Kit said, "Good goin', Darby. See ya later, I'm pickin' up some hay in town."

It wasn't long after he left that Darby felt Navigator's gait shift from smooth to choppy.

At first she blamed it on herself, but she was pretty sure she hadn't changed the way she was riding. She glanced at Megan, still standing at the rail, and noticed her friend frowning at the gelding's uneven steps.

When she came abreast of Jonah, Darby stopped the gelding.

"Something's wrong with Navigator," she told her grandfather.

Navigator nuzzled the front of Jonah's shirt, but he pushed the horse away.

"Keep him at a jog."

Darby swung Navigator away from Jonah, and urged the dark brown gelding into a jog around open-air arena.

She was bouncing more than usual in her saddle, so she tried not to watch as Hoku followed Navigator.

"It's not the horse," Jonah said as Darby rode past.

But it was. Maybe it was the muggy weather, or Hoku dogging his steps, but Darby knew Navigator's stiffness and the way he sawed his mouth against the bit was not her fault.

"I trained that gelding myself. It's either you or that broomtail," Jonah said, pointing.

"No way," Darby said. Trying to believe Jonah was joking, Darby smooched at Hoku as she and Navigator jogged past.

But Navigator wasn't joking. The Quarter Horse moved from a walk, to a jog, then a lope, at her command, but every gait felt as if his legs were jointless wood.

Jonah studied her riding position.

"He thinks he's bound for the racetrack, the way you're up on his neck like a jockey," Jonah told Darby. "Sit back."

"Okay," Darby said, and for a few seconds, she felt at home in the smooth leather seat. Maybe it had been her fault after all.

"Now, jog."

At once, Darby's teeth slammed together.

It was like Navigator's muscles resisted the movement of his bones.

Darby swiped at the sweat on her forehead.

Neither she nor Navigator could relax, and the April afternoon felt like it was holding its breath.

"Keep him on the fence," Jonah ordered.

Navigator's ears flicked back as Darby adjusted her reins.

"Good boy," Darby told him.

Hoku neighed and rushed from one side of the round pen to the other.

"Get centered. You're leaning left. Sit back." Jonah's voice was charged with frustration. "Ignore that filly."

She tried. She stared at the space between Navigator's ears instead of turning toward the thump of Hoku's hooves.

The next time she and Navigator swept by Jonah, her grandfather frowned.

"Stop," he said.

Darby's fingers flexed. Navigator halted.

Sunstruck dust motes turned gold all around them, but they only made Darby sneeze.

Jonah's black hair glinted silver at the temples and his stride was certain as he approached.

Navigator danced in place. He swung his head so that Darby could see the froth on his lips.

Jonah held up a hand and the gelding lowered his head.

Jonah walked around the horse. Starting at the hooves, moving up over fetlocks, bone and sinew, his analytical eyes examined each bulge and dip beneath glossy horse hide. He considered bridle straps and saddle buckles, and finally said, "Try holding a rein in each hand. Look down at your saddle horn."

"Okay."

Darby waited for Jonah to return to his place by the gate.

Her grandfather's back was as straight as if a steel rod lay along his spine. She wasn't sure what he was thinking. That she was the only Kealoha on earth not born to be a rider? That he shouldn't have gone along with Kit's idea to turn Hoku out into the round pen while they rode?

Or was he, just maybe, silently agreeing with her that something was disturbing the dependable Quarter Horse?

"Don't keep him going in circles. Pick a post across the arena and ride to it. Then do it again. Not the same place, though. Mix it up."

Darby tried, but the very first time she sighted a fence post and rode for it, the gelding wrenched his head to the right and came in sideways to the fence.

"Why'd you let him do that?" Jonah said incredulously.

Before Darby could answer, Navigator froze in place, ears pitched so far forward, Darby listened for whatever he heard.

Hoku was doing the same thing, and both horses shivered as if flies crawled over every inch of their skins.

"He's shaking," she told Jonah.

"Cluck him up. Put him into a lope and keep him there."

Navigator bounded forward, pretending he was about to lope, before breaking into a gallop.

Hoku joined him, running alongside so closely, her shoulder bumped Darby's stirrup. They were running too fast, slanting like motorcycles on a track.

Faintly, she heard Jonah's warning tone repeat, "Lope."

Head level, teeth ringing on the bit, Navigator began to buck.

Darby grabbed onto the saddle horn. The gelding's ragged breath was all around her when she fell forward on his neck. She didn't release her grip on the horn, even when it jabbed her ribs.

She stayed on long enough that Navigator stopped bucking, but he was running again, this time at a reeling, unsteady gait.

As the gelding homed in on a section of fence, she thought he was going to try to jump out of the round pen.

Then, Darby saw that she was wrong.

Good, steady Navigator was about to rub her off on the fence.

# Discover all the adventures on Wild Horse Island!

THE HORSE CHARMER
TERRI FARLEY

THE SHINING STALLION
TERRI FARLEY

RAIN FOREST ROSE
TERRI FARLEY

CASTAWAY COLT
TERRI FARLEY

FIRE MAIDEN
TERRI FARLEY

www.harpercollinschildrens.com